Born the youngest of seven, raised on a smallholding. Her childhood gave her the foundation to build a colourful life. She would never want for anything as she worked hard to make her money, knowing the deprivation she had come from, she was determined to live a loving and kind life with understanding and compassion for all.

To my biggest fan and best friend my Husband Giles Duckworth

To my children William, Thomas, and Summer Angel

Mrs. S A Platt – My mother, who flies in heaven.

My brothers and sisters, especially Martin James Platt, who died too early.

If I was to document every person who has touched my life, then this would be a very long list, however, here are just a few.

Mr A Mawdsley.

All the children and families at Rainbow House Charity.

Miss. Karen Colles & Miss. Hayley Scholes

Rainbow House staff, team and directors.

My primary school teacher Mrs. Swarbrick

My high school teacher Mrs. Cooper

Mrs. Blackburn

Mr. Robert Wright

A great mentor Mr. John Dewhurst of the Woodenspoon.

My childhood friends, you all know who you are.

Finally, two very special ladies who stand by me no matter what.

Mrs. Kathleen Spiby

Mrs. Charlotte Gilston.

J M Duckworth

MOLLY MEE
THE AWAKENING

AUSTIN MACAULEY PUBLISHERS™
LONDON · CAMBRIDGE · NEW YORK · SHARJAH

Copyright © J M Duckworth 2023

The right of J M Duckworth to be identified as author of this work has been asserted by the author in accordance with sections 77 and 78 of the Copyright, Designs and Patents Act 1988.

All rights reserved. No part of this publication may be reproduced, stored in a retrieval system, or transmitted in any form or by any means, electronic, mechanical, photocopying, recording, or otherwise, without the prior permission of the publishers.

Any person who commits any unauthorised act in relation to this publication may be liable to criminal prosecution and civil claims for damages.

This is a work of fiction. Names, characters, businesses, places, events, locales, and incidents are either the products of the author's imagination or used in a fictitious manner. Any resemblance to actual persons, living or dead, or actual events is purely coincidental.

A CIP catalogue record for this title is available from the British Library.

ISBN 9781398495937 (Paperback)
ISBN 9781398495944 (ePub e-book)

www.austinmacauley.com

First Published 2023
Austin Macauley Publishers Ltd®
1 Canada Square
Canary Wharf
London
E14 5AA

The biggest acknowledgement is to the universe who encouraged me to write this book. The book derived from many hours of channelling inner emotions and past experiences which I needed to face before I could ever move forward in life.

Therefor this acknowledgment is to every person who I have ever communicated with, to every person I have had an experience with, good or bad. This is to the people and life experiences I have had without whom this book was not possible, sincere thanks.

With sincere gratitude I thank every one of you, especially Austin Macauley book publishers who took a chance on me and published the book.

Introduction

From being young, I never quite fitted in; I always preferred to live in my head than face the world in which I had been born. To live in my bubble, one of fantasy and hope, where the impossible was possible, and where difference didn't matter, there was no judgement, no expectations; just love; this is the world I craved for, but life wasn't meant to be that way, life was dark, life was angry, leaving me wondering where was my life going to lead, how was I ever going to make it?

Self-doubt was all consuming, it was set deep into my soul, there was no one in the world who I trusted, I didn't even trust myself, even though I knew I was different, I never knew how different I was. Sometimes, I felt like I understood life and what it was about, telling myself that I had got this, I am going to be OK, but no sooner did I feel this way than I was pulled back to reality, and my reality was one of darkness where actual laughter and joy were rare occasions, shared with people I didn't belong with.

I have always found life like a long list of disappointments, let downs, which are created by fear. I hear you ask why fear? Well, this is what we pave the way with, fear; fear of being different, fear of not achieving, fear of not being like everyone else. Fears we think and feel everyday of our lives, instead of embracing them and welcoming them, supporting them to help mould us into the people we are meant to become, we allow them to control us, we act the same way as others, we follow like army ants, as no one dares to show their difference, I wonder why this is?

For generations, history has shown how difference is treated-hate, fear and punishment. The people who were perceived to have power or be different were burnt alive; those who could heal were deemed to be witches, hung, drowned and tortured; however, there were those few who hid their talents behind their afflictions, be them physical afflictions or mental, they were clever and used these to masquerade their abilities, as they were not deemed a threat as they weren't considered to have the ability to live, never mind achieve, but how wrong people were.

There is a long list of these people who throughout history achieved great things, they weren't feared, or thought to be gifted; they were outcasts in society, believed to be crazy or retarded. Take Einstein who suffered chronic illness, yet he discovered a theory of relativity, which revolutionised our understanding of space, time, gravity, and the universe. Vangogh who had epilepsy, yet painted masterpieces which are still sought after today; Michelangelo who suffered from arthritis, having limited function in his hands and feet, yet was the world's greatest painter and sculptor.

These people had great power, yet they were humble choosing to share their gift with the world through creation; they were not punished as they posed no threat, they were greatly underestimated at the time. Then they were revered, thank goodness no one felt threatened by these people; it would have been a crying shame if they were thought to have out of this world abilities, then put to death for their gifts.

Now, I'm no witch, but I do feel different, just don't ask me how, I just do, and every day, I fight to keep that little part of me alive; my difference is my tool, my difference is my saviour, and I don't even know why, but I'm sure we will soon find out.

Chapter 1

The place I call home, the place where I live, the place to which I was born, yet I didn't feel welcome, I did not fit in. Could it be that I was born into the wrong home, really? That is impossible, that's the most ludicrous thing I have even thought, but this home has a heart which is running on half measures, darkness and hate penetrates the wood, they are not the same as everyone else, they don't fit in, they are not a normal family, so it's not that. Yet they do seem to think that they are better than everyone else; they judge those who are less fortunate, even though they live in a chicken pen, but they are better, they are more worthy, they flaunt around in their designer clothes, use state of the art technology. They are a farming family of nine people, mother, father, four brothers, two sisters and me, that makes seven children.

We live on the outskirts of an up-and-coming village, where people's homes are dominated with affluence and keeping up with the Jones's, new houses being built everywhere, new cars and people going off to towns and cities doing proper jobs, then there was my home. A white cottage built in the early 1900s, nestled at the end of a country lane, the last house on the left, surrounded by sheds where cows, pigs and chickens shared their home with the people who lived there.

A mother who worked her fingers to the bone; a father who was never there and when he was, the world got darker; a cottage which was meant to be clean but was tired and worn, as was the lady who kept her. The children were angry and bitter, arguments every day, as they fought for clothes, food, or the TV. Whatever the reason, there were always harsh words spoken. The environment was not pleasant, and good times were rare, but it was home.

As I entered the cottage, the porch way had boots scattered all over the floor, causing me to trip, just saving myself in time, so as I didn't create noise, as noise always meant the jibes and the hurt, all right weirdo, you're a freak, and on and on it went. Sometimes, I just want to tell them to look in the mirror, but I don't; they look in the mirror a million times a day anyway and it doesn't make them look any nicer or act any nicer. Anyhow, I have averted that outbreak; they cannot say anything to me, as I have not done anything wrong.

Wrong, how wrong was I, no sooner in the door, "Have you taken my bra? My bra has gone missing, and you have it, let me see!" I was horror struck and she tore at my sweater trying to see what was under it, the sweater ripped, and I stood in all my glory, no t-shirt, no vest, and no bra. Oh, she scowled and off she went, leaving me bare , no doubt I was going to get scolded for that too, I had better mend it before anyone notices. In the front room was a three-piece settee, a TV and a fire. The open fire took pride of place in the centre of the room, warming its dark soul, then emanating to the sofas and TV, at either side of the fire were brass buckets and within one were wool balls and needles, I set to work mending my sweater before mother saw it.

I threaded the needle with green wool; the wool was too thick, and the hole wasn't big enough, so I had to wet it slightly by a quick touch of the lips, engrossed in threading the needle, I didn't notice mother. There she stood, right at the side of me, "What are you doing?" She scolded. "What have you broken now?"

"Nothing." I replied, I'm just mending my sweater, as I darned as quickly as I could, "Just something else that I'm going pay for hey," my mother's eyes darted to me, "You need to find a job and start paying your own way." I was fourteen years old and had a paper round and didn't ask for anything; I had hand-me-down clothes and my God, the food I ate or didn't eat, what did she 'actually' pay for me? I just replied, "Yes, mother," as hurt burned inside. Tears started to well in my eyes, as she looked at me and scolded some more.

"Don't you dare cry, tears won't help you." I knew if the tears fell, then the back of her hand I would feel, I can sense the smarting on my ace from the smack which was yet to come. I looked away in the hope that she wouldn't notice, the pain in my chest as it contracted, I found it hard to breath, but I couldn't cry; then wham, my face burnt, the handprint reddened my face and tears fell silently, nothing more was said, and she walked away.

I finished the sweater, maybe no one would notice, I think I made a pretty good darner, not something recognised today, but for me, it was saviour. I had learnt how to darn from an elderly lady that lived in the terraced house at the end of our lane. Her house was old, but sturdy, made of brick and slate, taking pride of place at the side of the village green and watching over the village school which was directly opposite. The house was warm and inviting, it seemed to glow with a loving energy, you entered the house via the back door; to the right of the door was a coal house, in front of you was the pantry with a small toilet tucked in the right corner behind a heavy red door; in the pantry herbs hung from the ceiling, as they dried, to make whatever it was she made, shelves were packed with jars which had homemade lids, tied with green twine, there wasn't a tin in sight. There were no Heinze beans, no HP sauce; everything in this pantry was made by Bell's hand. The house had a faint smell of lavender, which set the calmness to this wonderful house which I was invited into.

Bell was a kind lady, she was extremely small and frail, her bones never looked strong enough to carry her, yet they did; even though she stood at four foot ten, her energy made her look bigger, her kindness radiated, and her words of wisdom warmed me and made me feel protected. I spent many hours with Bell, as I tended her garden; albeit a very small garden, it was well maintained where she grew herbs and fruit, the branches were always laden; this is where I found comfort, at one with nature. In return for my assistance, Bell taught me how to sew and darn, she was amazing with a needle, and did not even need glasses, even though she seemed very old. I think Bell would be happy with the quality of my darning.

As I stood to leave the front room, in came my brother; Erbie (short for Erbert) was the middle of the children, he was very quiet and rarely spoke, he was constantly sad and didn't seem to have any happiness within him, he looked at me and said nothing, but in his eyes, I could see that he felt sorry for me. I did not want his pity; I just wanted it to stop. I wanted a normal life, one where I was loved and where I could join in conversations without reprimand; I felt like I had so much inside, but was always too afraid to speak the words. *When was this life ever going to get better? Was this the life that was planned out for me, a life of sadness, a life of hurt and pain, what kind of mother would that make me? Would I ever be a mother?*

The self-doubt stepped back in, and my chest tightened again making it hard to breath; oh no, was I going to cry again, I cannot let them see me. The tears stung my eyes and I tried so hard not to cry, so the tears fell inside, an inconsolable flood of tears raged through my body as I walked out of the room and into the hallway. The hall was about twenty-foot-long and a meter wide, the walls were damp, rotting the skirting boards and discolouring the plaster. As it rotted, the plaster softened and fell as fine white dust on the wooden floor. This didn't make the wooden floor look that bad, in fact, it probably enhanced it, as the floor was already laden with muck of people's shoes, the white dust made it look somewhat prettier.

No one had much pride in housekeeping, mother tried, but it was always in vain, no sooner was it tidy, then it was dirty from mucky wellies and boots, all sorts were trampled in animal dirt; feathers, shavings, and straw were scattered here and there and odd cigarette stumps which had been trod on many times were stuck to the wood. My father didn't have any pride, he never wiped his feet, nor cared about what his boots brought in, it didn't matter where he finished his cigarette, he would put it out anywhere, be it the hall, bathroom or kitchen, but mother had rules about the living room, there were ashtrays and a fire and she made certain there were no cigarette stumps in there, and if a stump was found on the carpet, then holy hell would be let loose.

They say *home is where the heart is*, well my heart is somewhere else, I don't know where, but it isn't here, in fact I don't think there is any heart here, just a bunch of people trying to survive, a bunch of people who have been thrown together and someone out there is watching how they all do. *Is this a test, is this the will of the fittest, or fastest? My God, I haven't got a clue what it is, maybe its hell and I am living in purgatory, maybe it's just life, nothing more nothing less, maybe there isn't anything more to life. Birth leads to what? Hurt, pain, loss, and disappointment?*

At the end of the hallway is a newish door, made of plywood, thin and flimsy. It's the only odd door in the house; all the other doors are solid and heavy, but this one is made of man's materials. As I step through the door, I enter the room we call the lounge. The lounge was added onto the house in 1996, this was when the eldest was born, she is now 24years old and now I'm 14, so it's been here 24 years. The room was added to give additional bedroom space, but it never quite made it. It's a large room with a low roof but leaves a light and airy feel. During the summer months, this room soaked up the summer sun and retained its warmth for all to enjoy, but in the autumn and winter months, the room is hardly used. There is one radiator heating the entire room; however, the radiator only ever works when the fire is lit, and that is normally at night time, leaving the beautiful room without heat all day.

There was an old electric fire surround which stood central to the room, it housed the old brasses of gypsies, with golden goblets and hanging horse shoes, yet the fire was rarely used, as father said it cost too much money to pay for the electric, so the beautiful lounge which shone in the summer, was left to hibernate in the winter months, making it the ideal room for me to use, as no one else dared go in, even though the three bedrooms were shared, the boys had their rooms and the girls had one big bedroom upstairs, it left little room for privacy, so peace and quiet was my respite, and this room gave me solace.

Even though the room was cold, it still had the warmth and energy of the past summer, as we slipped slowly into autumn; the room had yet to slumber completely into the winter hibernation, so this was the room where I charged up my batteries, this was the room I explored in, this was the room where my imagination ran wild and broke free of the limitation and confines of this supposed home. This was the room where I read J K Rowling, and the adventures of Harry Potter, The Hobbit and much more.

All the books had one commonality-there was hope, and kindness; they helped me to imagine a better world where magic ruled. The books did tell of trials and tribulations, but they gave you the hope that you would and could overcome these, and those loving arms would be there to hold and reassure you that everything would be OK. Not like real life at all, but hopefully it was making me the person who I dreamt I would always be, one day I would leave the confines of pain, hurt and disappointment.

I never felt the cold as my mind was taken on an adventure, where anything was possible and the impossible was conquered, so therefore the lounge was a great place for me to be, well that was until now. The door handle creaked, and under the weight, it was flung open. In came my brother looking for his jeans, he always had something to find, maybe if he actually tidied things away, he would be able to find them far easier, but he doesn't, so at least once a day, he has a total meltdown and creates havoc in an already unstable home. I sat as quiet as could be, barely breathing in the hope that he would not notice me curled up on the sofa, I hid the book I was reading down the side of the sofa, so as he could say nothing. As he was screaming out, "Who has got my jeans, where the hell are they?"

The jeans lay in the pile of washing which had been brought back from the laundry a couple of days earlier, I could see them in the pile, but he wasn't even looking there. He was just throwing things about and covering the floor with towels and tees. Would he ever learn, that if he calmed and just looked, then all would be revealed, but this is Arty we are talking about, he is a force of nature, one whom will consume, not be consumed, one who will hurt without thought, one who will get through life with manipulation and whispered words.

Arty was five foot nothing, a rounded fuller figure with a mop of straight brown hair which framed his face, beady eyes resting above his hook nose, skin pale and mottled with past acne scars. Arty had a towel which barley covered his hips, not leaving much to the imagination, but he wasn't bothered as his confidence in his external appearance was one of exuberance and ego. Arty's rounded torso sat on top of thin, skinny legs, a belly which hung over the hips and a frame which could not be seen due to additional fat which covered it. But he thought he looked amazing and was in constant competition with his brother Jay who was the complete opposite. Arty was grunting and squealing like a pig, as he scurried through the pile looking for jeans which really did nothing to aid his figure.

His face was reddening, as he got madder and madder looking for the jeans which were right in front of his nose, he finally found them and left the room, never bothering to pick up the clean clothes which he had thrown on the dirty floor, covering them in straw and shavings. I sighed a breath of relief as he left the room, feeling quite glad that he had not noticed me sat there. Relieved that he had not seen me, I started to work gathering the clothes and folding them neatly before mother found them on the floor.

The door opened again, I froze in anticipation, if it was mother, then no doubt there would be another smack for me, as she wouldn't stop and listen to the justification of why the clothes were on the floor, but it wasn't mother; my body tightened as I felt the dark energy enter; it was Nessa, way worse than mother. In fact, she was a younger version of mother, with her slim demeanour, olive skin, button nose, big green eyes, high cheekbones and perfect teeth. Nessa began with her usual, what are you doing freak, why are you throwing clothes around, they have just been washed, and no sooner had the words been said then her trademark look came, her pouted lips pursed as she struck out, launching a punch right in my ribs, for a slim teen, she didn't half pack a punch.

My breath got stuck as I found it hard to breath, she had winded me some, as I was hurled onto the floor, the punches kept coming, the words along with them, "Go back to the children's home where you came from, you don't belong here. I am going to tell mum what you are doing, weirdo," and with that, she stormed out leaving the room with a pungent smell of stale perfume and cigarettes.

Nessa was probably the worst of them all, she really thought she was someone, she dated a wealthy young man who lived in a luxurious house, and wore designer clothes, but he didn't know what she was like, he didn't know the darkness which lay beneath her, he was blinded and unable to see her for what she was. I got myself together and finished folding the clothes, when in came mother. Mother said nothing, and walked out with a sigh, reassured by her lack of interest, I left the room and closed the door, leaving the room in the state I found it. No sooner had I entered the hallway than bam, my head swirled as I had to catch myself, I did not see that coming, I did not see her. Mother had been in the toilet doorway, her hand had reach out and smacked me right across the head, shaking my brain. I was dazed and speechless, I thought she had nothing to say, I thought I had saved the day by folding the clothes which Arty had thrown on the floor. I thought I had averted the wrath of mother, but no. Nessa stood behind her sniggering as my vision returned, I said nothing, no tears fell and that was a normal day.

My life, what was it? I did not know why these people who I was born too scorned me so much, I did not know where my life would go, or if I would even have a life, this was no life. I constantly wished for my life to end, as I told myself I was not good enough, and the world would be a better place without me. Why did they even have me, I really do not know. My mother constantly reminded me that I wasn't wanted, and that it was because of me that she could have no more children, why would she even want any more children, she can't manage with the ones she has got, but that didn't matter to her, she just seemed to like the fact that this was held over me.

When my mother was pregnant, she developed a cyst in her ovaries, the cyst grew large and they told her to have an abortion, but she wouldn't. I don't know why, it's not as if she is catholic or even religious, so why she wouldn't just get rid, made no sense to me. Why did she have to be a martyr, she carried the baby inside until she could carry it no longer and the doctors said it was time to give birth; 11 minutes past 11 in the morning on the 11 November, I was born, 11:11 some say that this date is of relevance, the seventh child born on the 11th day of the 11th Month, well not for me.

I was brought into the world three months early, at only 2lb weight, and was lucky to be alive, my mother was then rushed to a hospital in the capital where they performed lifesaving surgery on her, leaving me in a hospital nursery to be cared for by the beautiful nurses. I was in hospital alone for three months. My mother got great satisfaction taunting me telling me no one came to see me, my mother was recovering, and the nurses cared for me, until the day I finally went home.

My mother constantly reminds me of this event, as if I could do anything about it? I was a baby, she was in control, she could have aborted, no one would have known any difference, then she would have had the operation and been able to have more babies, well at least, that is what she tells me. The Mee family was already big enough, my mother's maiden family were Spencer's, she was one of eleven and my father was from an old Irish family, one of five. They had all expanded with children and grandchildren, and even great grandchildren, so the Spencer name lived on, so why was I born again, why did they 'actually' need another?

My mother never lets me forget the day I was born, constantly reminding me that I wasn't welcome, constantly telling me that I wasn't wanted, you were trouble from the day you were born she would scold, in my head I used to think that I was survivor from the day I was born, but they don't see that. So, I continue to survive, but survive for what, what is life 'really' about?

Dinner was served and I sat in my usual place perched on the end of a wooden bench which was pushed against a wall, and at the side of my mother, why I ever started sitting there, I do not know, but that was my place. It would be a long time until I could ever advance to a chair, there were eight dining that night, my eldest sister Immy was out with her boyfriend, she was about the nicest sister I had, she was the kindest of them all. Her face was warm and her eyes caring, her soft brown curls which fell to the shape of her perfectly formed face, I always missed her when she wasn't there. Immy (short for Imogen) would normally sit directly opposite me, a face of reassurance, she was the only one in this family who cared anything for me, but soon, she would be gone, as her marriage plans were underway and soon the big day would come, and she will leave. I wasn't looking forward to that day, even though I was being her bridesmaid, I feared how I would manage at home, maybe she would take me with her, maybe?

I ate in silence, head down looking directly at the plate, there were two potatoes hard boiled, which were covered in barley and lentils, with a little bit of greenery in there, the juice was transparent and watery, it was bland and flavourless, there was no chicken stock or anything to taste, because there was no chicken, the pieces of meat were rabbit or hare. You always knew when these were to be served, one because they would no longer hang in the porch and two because she would always try to mask the meat in a stew; the rabbit was darker than chicken, and had a strange taste, not like chicken at all, the texture was stringy and always got stuck in my teeth. I really didn't like it, but there was no point in complaining, and I had already had a lot of smacks today, so wasn't about to get another one.

I ate the stew and then had some bread and butter to fill up my belly; the dinners never filled me, there was barely enough to feed a dwarf, never mind growing children, but there was always pudding. All sorts of puddings were made, apple pie, gooseberry, blackcurrant and more, sometimes there was rice pudding or egg custard, for some reason, she never spared on the puddings, so tonight, it was rice pudding, which I have to say was delicious. I ate with speed and soon emptied my bowl, my brother who was sat beside me did the same, as we finished, we both chuckled, I think that was the first smile I had all day, and it felt good. Fin was ten months older than me, he was the same height, a slight frame with big blue eyes and blonde hair, he always had a slight grin on his face, which showed his dimple, Fin was my confident, whilst Immy was the protector, Fin was the only other person I trusted in this family. As we smiled, we could see our nemesis scowling at us, Jay and Arty. Jay wasn't really the enemy, but his relationship with his piggy brother was all what was required to forge a distrust of him, hence we kept him at arm's length.

Jay was the spoilt child, he could never do anything wrong, whatever he wanted he got, and if he didn't get it, then a tantrum he would have. Jay was the middle child, and I have to say, the most handsome, six foot two, soft blond locks, olive skin, a perfectly formed body, muscular and taut, there wasn't an ounce of fat on him. He was the envy of all the boys at school, and could have had any girl he liked, but he was easily led and Arty never let him stray too far, except something tells me that he would go further than any brother. Jay is beautiful, both inside and out. Arty knows this and somehow fears it, so he keeps Jay close, he takes him out clubbing and to parties; somehow, I feel that Arty despises Jay. Nevertheless, Jay uses Arty for his car and to escape the home life. Arty needs Jay because Jay gets all the attention with his handsome looks and kind manner.

It's all mind games and manipulation in this group I call family. I hope one day Jay will see the error of his ways and break free from Arty's hold. The darkness and jealousy which resides in Arty is far worse than anything Jay can imagine. Don't be misled by their arrangement, I don't think that they are friends, each fulfils a need of the other and one day, their paths will part. They will both live the lives they were destined for, just something tells me that Jays will be a little less manipulative than Arty's.

As Jay and Arty got up, they started to empty the table, clearing the dirty plates and bowls, leaving them on the side for me and Fin to wash and put away, we knew our place, this was common practice, a nightly ritual which we conformed to without question, without hesitation, as to hesitate would certainly mean a smack for being defiant, and that wasn't in my remit tonight. So, every plate, bowl and piece of cutlery was cleaned and scrubbed, then put away, the kitchen was left spotless, and I was then able to go into the front room and watch TV. This was the norm, everyone sits together and watch coronation street, then it would be bed, it was like living in the 1960s but this was the modern era 2019.

This evening, there were only the four of us, Immy was out with her boyfriend, Arty and Jay were out on the town and well Erbie, he was probably driving around in his car, doing God knows what, no one really knows what he does, whether he has friends or no friends, no one ever sees him with anyone. Yet he is out most of the time, if he isn't working at the farm down the road, or on the milk round, he is out, rarely do we see him during the day.

The living room was cosy, as the small fire roared and kept us warm, the wind shook the side door and slight breeze wafted through every now and again, which was refreshing. The TV was in the far corner of the room, to the right of the window, which looked onto next doors fence, and Mrs F's garden. To the left of the window was a rocking chair, which no one ever used, then my mother's chair, a small table where she had her ash tray and a cup of tea, then another chair, a small walkway where you entered from the hall and a three-seater sofa in the recess under the stairs.

The room was small but snug with two wall lights either side of the fire, dimly lighting the room, my seating place was leaning against the sofa, where my short legs could rest on the fire burnt rug. My father was sprawled on the sofa leaving little room for anyone else, Fin was on the middle chair, which was not his normal resting place, as he would normally be huddled at the side of the fire, but tonight he seemed chilled and was happily watching his favourite program. Coronation street came to end, then off to bed we went, we didn't need to be told, we just went. Fin said goodnight, mother and father grunted as we left the room.

Fin said, "Night night, God bless, Molly, see you when the cocks crow." He was always coming out with silly things, I smiled and said, "OK, night night." I made certain I went to the toilet before bed, as the bedroom was dark, there was only one main light which you had to walk to other end of the room to switch on, there were no lamps, no radios, no nothing in our rooms; there was no personality, which made it stark and hostile.

I clicked the door and stepped up onto the first step, the stairs were enclosed with one light in the middle. The top of the stairs there were two doors, the one to the left which was the girl's room and the one in front which was Arty's and Jays. I opened our door, it was quiet and smelled of dampness and body odour, the room was situated right above the living room and had the chimney breast run through it, so you would think it would be somewhat warmer and more inviting, but it wasn't. The room always made me shudder and the urge to run to my bed was prevalent. I flipped the light switch and hurriedly climbed into bed.

My bed was in front of the window, which was somewhat breezy, and the window frame was rotten and let in every whisp of air. Nessa slept opposite me near the stairs and Immy slept in the alcove near the chimney breast. My bed was old and bumpy, with indents in the mattress, so I perched on the side. You would think that I would enjoy having the bedroom all to myself, but when Immy wasn't here, the room felt full of hurt and pain, or was that just me?

Chapter 2

Normally, it takes me a while to get to sleep; as I lay there thinking of the day's events, and the reprimands I have had, usually I would torture myself and tell myself how bad I am, and that I really need to change, but not this night, even though the day had been eventful, I was soon fast asleep. I didn't hear Nessa come to bed, but I felt her presence in the middle of the night, as the energy had grown darker, as I was awoken by a faint, "I am here, where are you, I've come to take you, out of the blue."

I dare not open my eyes, had red clogs come to finally take me away? Was this my time? Red Clogs were the spirit in the attic room; just off the bedroom was an airing cupboard which housed a water storage tank heated by the fire downstairs, there were some shelves where bedding was stored, and old boxes stored around the outside. At the side of the boiler, there was an old brick wall and a small door which led into the eaves, it was dark and full of cobwebs, no one ever went in there, I had only been in once and it wasn't by choice. Sometimes, I would hear a faint tapping in the attic, Nessa said it was Red Clogs, a man who used to work in the weaving mill, he took his own life, because his true love had married another.

I don't know if this was true, but I did feel a presence. I never felt that it was bad, or that it was going to harm me, so I dismissed it. If this was the night that Red Clogs chose to show himself then that would be fine with me, maybe I would have a heart attack if I saw him and then I would die, I welcome that day, so my body relaxed and I felt at peace, in the hope that this was the day.

As I was dozing, the chant came again, "I am here, where are you? I've come to take you out of the blue." It was friendly chant, one of hope and love, I felt the warmth of the chant and replied, "I am here, I am ready for you to take me, please take me." With that, I was suddenly in a beautiful green meadow, the sweet smell of summer grass and wildflowers which swayed in the breeze, the sun was warm on my face, the sweet aroma filled my lungs, I was no longer in my dark dank bedroom, I was free. I had been transported to another place, one filled with love and happiness.

I spread my arms as I ran through the meadow, my feet plunging into the soft grass, each step was welcomed, my heart was free, I felt amazing. I*s this what it is like to be dead, is this what heaven is like? Oh, my God, I want to stay. Thank you for answering my prayers, thank you for taking me this evening, thank you*. As I was happily singing my thanks, I saw colours exiting the woodland which lay on the edge of the meadow, all the colours of the rainbow, reds, oranges, pinks, blues, violet, indigo, yellow, the colours were vibrant, and full of love, I ran towards them, hoping that I could become a colour too, but as I got closer, I could see the faint out lines, they were body shapes, lots of body shapes, there were big ones, small ones, fat ones thin ones, all different sizes which seem bizarre.

As I edged closer, I could see that they were people, but they did not have faces, instead they had the face shape, the eyes were merely shadows, as were the lips, no ears, noses, or hair you would think that this would make them look weird, but it didn't, their faces were friendly, they made me feel safe.

"Welcome." I heard one of them say, I could not see who had said it, as their lips didn't move, "Thank you." I heard myself say with a big smile. "Where am I?"

"You are in Havenmoor."

"So, am I dead?"

"No, you are not dead, it is not yet your time."

I was confused, "What do you mean? I don't understand where Havenmoor is."

"Havenmoor is the place where all the souls reside prior to birth or rebirth, this is where you were born from." My head was spinning, I couldn't quite grasp what was being said to me, I'm either dead or I am dreaming, I wished it was the latter, but obviously not.

"So, let me get this right, I'm not dead? Am I dreaming then?" I could feel their laughter. "No you are not dreaming." *My goodness it's like a hundred questions, how am I ever going to get straight answer?*

And so, the story began. Let me take you back to when the world began, the Big Bang created earth, the microorganisms created creatures, soon man was created and so with the world, but man is just flesh and blood, the souls are consciousnesses and came from an alternate place, another planetary system, the souls which are born to earth rest here on Havenmoor. It is here that the souls come to from the other planets who have chosen to experience life as a human and be born, to go onto the earth plane to fulfil their birth plan or participate in the grand plan. In doing so then they are better able to ascend and live in eternal peace and harmony; it is only when they have achieved all their life goals that they are able to do this.

I was trying to take all of what was said in, but my simple brain was having great difficulty. Ascend? What on earth did they mean?

"Ascend means to never visit earth again, ascend means to live as the life's source of the world."

"So, you mean that once I have achieved all my goals, I can go to heaven?"

"Well, there are many names for it, and yes, heaven is one of them, but the actual word is the Source, the home you originated from."

I thought this would be easy; I heard the chant, I welcomed it, I expected to die, not be here in the alternate universe, it's like something of the X Files. For those of you who have never see the X Files, it's a TV series which tells tales of extra-terrestrial beings, yes, you have got it, Aliens, little green men, they enter the world and Mulder and Scully are always looking for ways to show the world that these beings are real, my goodness, they should be here with me, they would love this. Maybe I wasn't meant to die, maybe that whack on the head tonight has sent me mad, maybe I should go to a loony asylum, this isn't real; I have exceeded myself, my imagination has got the better of me and yes, I have cracked up, the yellow van will come to take me away tomorrow.

I could feel my eyes widen, as they spoke. "Listen, my sweet child, let me reassure you, this is real, this is very real,

Havenmoor is in need, something is happening with the souls, with the light, with the energy, and we need help."

"But I don't understand why me?"

"You are one of the oldest souls on the earth at this time, this was to be your last visit to earth, then you would ascend, there is no one more experienced with the earth people than you."

My mind was working overtime, what on earth did they mean, I have never been to this place before, and I sure as hell don't remember living on earth before, why would anyone ever choose to go to that hell hole, what lessons could those people ever teach these beautiful souls here? I couldn't think straight, I knew I was different, I knew I had a path, but how did I know? Oh, my goodness, this is all too complicated, this is absurd.

"So, let me get this straight, I used to exist here, this was my home, then for some ludicrous reason, I chose to enter a body on earth and be reborn, forgetting all of this, forgetting where I came from? That simply doesn't make sense. Why would I choose to leave here, what happens to the souls who don't ever want to be reborn?"

"We know this is a lot to take in, but all the souls who rest here, are here for a short time, until they are reborn, there is a timescale of a thousand galactic years which you can stay at Havenmoor, then you must be reborn to fulfil your life's path."

"What if you never fulfil your life's path, what if you never achieve your goal, and who even decides what your path is?"

The calmness in the reply was eerie, and one which I didn't want to hear, but I knew it was coming. "You choose the goal, you choose the path, then you spend lifetimes trying to achieve that goal, only when the goal has been achieved can you ascend."

"I can understand that we set the goal, but when is this goal set, and why can't I remember it?"

"The life's goal is set on your first birthing, but then each time you are birthed, you set personal growth goals, or life changing goals."

"So, how old am I, in the soul world?" Now I could see their faces, well not quite faces, but changes of expression as I asked the question.

"Are you going to answer?"

My body was tightening and squirming under the stillness of anticipation, "Why aren't you answering?"

"You are as old as time, you have spent 360 lifetimes on earth, some long, some short, this is your last lifetime, then you are to ascend."

My stomach flipped, I must have been really rubbish on earth the past times too, this is too much, I am an elder, I have never achieved my goal in 360 lifetimes. Who says I will achieve it in this lifetime? How can they be certain that I will ascend, how can they be certain that I won't spend another 360 lifetimes? My heart was aching, what had I done, what kind of person must I be, I have failed in 360 lifetimes, do I 'actually' deserve to ascend, maybe what people say about me is true, maybe I am a freak, and I will always remain a freak.

"Master, apologies we misled you, we told you of the normal process, but your process has been slightly different, you have had the opportunity to ascend many times. But you have chosen not to, as you felt your time would better spent on earth, helping and progressing man, you have had many achievements, but these have taken their toll, you have sacrificed much."

"So, why is this my last lifetime, why now?"

"This was your choice, you made this decision before leaving to be birthed, but then your birth was rushed, and we didn't have time to plan what your actual goal was for this life; therefore, you have no goal, no mission, you were meant to enjoy and witness, but we need you and we need you to awaken."

"Really! I cannot call my experience enjoyment; its hell, I have felt lost and alone, my heart aches constantly and I just want to die, so if I die do, I come back here, then I can ascend?"

I could feel the look of concern, "If you take your own life and die, then you go to the other realm where they will assess the damage, make certain changes and maybe one day return here, but unlikely. So, please don't think that it's so easy, you can't orchestrate an accident and die, and you can't take you own life."

Oh, my shoulders slumped, and a wave of hopelessness fell over me. How was I supposed to live this life? I could just exist and do nothing, wait until the day I die, then I can ascend and will never have to come back to earth again, yes that's what I will do. I perked up and felt a little better about the decision I had made. When.

"Master, we need you, this is unprecedented what we are now doing, this is not the normal process, but we need you to awaken and remember." I felt their apprehension.

"What do you need me to remember?" I didn't know what they wanted of me.

"You are an elder, a Master of the Pleiadeans born from Havenmoor; you are one of the oldest souls on earth at this time." I could hear their words resonating through my brain, but I felt nothing, surely if I was the Master of old, then I would have some recollection of the past, why had I decided to return to earth, why did I not ascend, why? So many questions, yet no reply, I couldn't feel or hear their words.

They all gathered around me, awaiting the answer, but I had nothing. I had no wisdom, I had no words of comfort, yet they looked to me for guidance. I don't remember any of this world, maybe if I had then things would be different, maybe if I knew why I was going to earth, I would have a chance of making the decision, but I didn't, so what now?

The calmness washed over me, and my body pulsed, I could feel the beating of my heart, the sensation of blood was running though my veins, my energy was raised, and my body began to vibrate, yet I was not scared. I didn't fear this; I welcomed it, I was returning home, I was returning to the light energy I was before.

I let the process happen, I didn't fight it, as I knew this was the way. This was the way I was going to awaken, and one day remember. Sheer happiness flooded every cell, I was free; free from the confines of the body, my soul was unrestricted and burnt bright in the beautiful green meadow. My colour was blue, and shone as bright as the sunlit sky, as it did so, six other light people came to my side, and we made the circle of seven.

I was at peace, my heart was full, my energy was boundless; I just wanted to run through the fields, explore the land, and stay here forever. Nothing else mattered, I finally felt peace; I had no bodily confinements, and this was me, pure energy. I ran as fast as I could leaving my people behind, the meadow was illuminous green radiating with energy, each blade of grass, every petal, every leaf was pulsating, the energy was unmistakably addictive.

I entered the forest without thought, the trees grew tall, the canopy of leaves blocked out the sunlight, leaving rays shining through at intermittent stages, illuminating the woodland floor, the energy in here was even more powerful. The forest floor was the cleanest floor I had ever seen, no fallen leaves, no broken branches, just a soft mulch floor where flowers thrived nourished by the love of the soil. I saw the path which lay ahead, guided by the light through the broken canopy, and followed it with an inner calmness.

My feet no longer touched the floor, as I glided, no body, just pure energy, it was amazing. I wonder if this is what the monks feel like when they meditate, is this where they come to, is this why they spend so much time in prayer, or are they just looking for answers like me? We had been learning about religions in school, I attended a Church of England school, and had been raised a Christian. I didn't attend the C of E Sunday school; I attended the Methodist Sunday School, not because my family was religious, it was just a way of them getting rid of us for a while. That was about the only Christian trait, other than attending a church school, I hadn't even been baptised, so what was Christian about me, but apparently, I'm a Christian.

The scriptures were taught, and Jesus was brought into my life, some of the stories were good and some were a little farfetched. I preferred the sermons which our Methodist minister delivered beautifully, it was a lady minister, and she was lovely, kind, and gentle, with a big heart. Her sermons were full of possibility and hope, leaving you to believe that you could achieve anything, everyone was equal, and everyone was loved, there was no judgement, just unconditional love. I enjoyed going to Sunday School, every Sunday morning at 10 am, we were given 50 pence for the collection tray, and set on our way, no parents, no chaperones just me and Fin on our merry way.

We were always made to feel welcome at our small Methodist chapel. The church seemed to blend into the village perfectly, made of large blocks of stone, with stained glass windows displaying the colours of the rainbow, protected by huge oak doors which were solid and secure, keeping unwanted visitors out. This little church was a haven, as we entered the doors the smell of must, would fill your lungs, even though this wasn't really a nice smell, it was a fragrance which always made me feel safe and warm.

The minister would greet us with a tender welcome, and a gentle pat on the shoulder, her touch was sincere, and filled with love, which I greatly appreciated. The church would hum with silent excited speech as they would catch up on what had happened in their lives the previous week, this would be their gossip, their social time, we were always accepted here, no discrimination, or looks of distaste, just acceptance.

As the church settled and the minister took her stand, we would take our seats and await our cue to go into Sunday School, but before that, we would sing uplifting and joyful songs, supported by the heavenly choir who must have practiced a lot, as they sang their angelic chords. I loved the Methodist chapel, even though it wasn't the most popular church in our village, none of our friends went to the

Methodist church, they went to the Church of England or Catholic churches.

Even though our village was small, it had all three churches, which told you something about the acceptance of the village, it embraced all kinds of people, religions, and beliefs; it was a great village to grow up in, even though it did have its grumps, majority of the people were hard working, but nice. The churches were there for everyone to enjoy, but I never quite felt at home in any of the others. The churches sat at either end of the village, the Church of England to the north and the Catholic to the south; they stood tall and proud, like bodyguards at either side of a door, guarding the village.

I sometimes went to the C of E Church with school; the church was imposing, standing in its own grounds on the edge of the village, just before the hump backed bridge at the side of a flowing river. The entrance to the church grounds was grand with a huge oak Lynch Gate, four posts with a slate roof, solid stone slabs at either side. You entered under the small canopy, through a double gate, which led you down a long stone path hidden by the large oaks, leading to a large opening in the wooded area. Here, stood the church in all her glory, she was really quite beautiful, as the sun settled on her imposing stance; however, the sermons did not portray the look of the building, as for me they were filled with control and judgement.

The church was impressive, but the energy never quite felt the same as the Methodist church, no minister there to greet you, just a churchman who would hand you the hymn book, then leave you to find your seat; as you sat, the whole congregation would turn and watch, there were few welcoming smiles, just a building with rows of wooden pews where people would sit awaiting the wise guidance of their vicar, but that rarely ever came.

The sermons weren't delivered with light, love, and energy; they were delivered with stories from the newspapers, or what was going on in today's society, negative news, which made you feel worse when you came out than when you went in. The commandments which were recited, or more dictated to you, leaving a sinful sense of failure. I didn't much like the commandments, as I didn't feel they served much purpose in today's society, other than controlling people to think as they thought, to insert their beliefs into the minds of men, to make men their followers, but how can these words inspire me to be good, to do good and feel good?

- You shall have no other Gods before me.
- You shall not make idols.
- You shall not take the name of the Lord your God in vain.
- Remember the sabbath day, keep it holy.
- You shall not murder.
- You shall not commit adultery.
- You shall not steal.
- You shall not bare false witness against your neighbour.
- You shall not covet/want/desire.

The commandments apparently originated from some stone tablets which were given to Moses by form of two stone tablets, but who translated them? Whose depiction was truth and has the true meaning of the commandments been lost in translation? Many scholars over time have asked this very question but will anyone truly know what was meant for man, other than the creators themselves.

Do the commandments have any place in society today? They are a tad outdated and extremely hypocritical. Though shalt not covet (desire), yet from day one, desire has been documented. Take Adam and Eve, for example, the first man and woman, in the Garden of Eden, they were told not to eat the forbidden fruit from the tree of knowledge of good and evil, yet they did, and were exiled from Eden.

We had been taught about many religions and their rituals, but what we hadn't been taught was where religion came from. Remembering the commandments sent sadness over me and my energy dulled a little. Is it possible for mankind to follow these commandments, or to abide by them? They are constant sinners, if what they do is sin, but if Adam and Eve were judged so harshly never to return to the garden of Eden, how is mankind meant to succeed, if this is how man was created?

The sermons made me feel like I was a bad person, like I wasn't good enough, but wow if he could see me now, a beautiful aura of pastel blue and gold, with pure love. The recollections of the religious journey I had experienced now enlightened me, as these memories served purpose. The way mankind was going, they were not going to survive, they were going to burn out. I had survived for 14 years on earth and every other day, I prayed for it to end. I prayed for my life to end, I didn't want to be there anymore, not that I ever wanted to be there, why did I ever choose to go back, would I ever remember why I chose earth over ascension?

The visions of the past filled my mind, the killings the murders, the hate and hurt, I could see and feel all fragmented versions. Where was it coming from? From the beginning of time, man has tried to control man, religion, politics, fashion food and even the arts, all want an element of control over the man's mind, so is man ever able to make a conscious choice, is man ever able to be truly free?

I could feel the sadness of man, maybe that's what I felt whilst on earth, maybe the control was too much. I was a mere child on earth, trying to find my way through a mass jungle of hurt and pain, a wilderness which was unforgiving and too challenging to imagine, obstacles in the way at every junction, no way to turn, foliage blocking your way and you couldn't see what was in front of you, whether it was a beautiful fruit tree or a serpent. There was no way out, no matter what path was taken there were dangers and untold truths, man searched and searched, but remains lost in the jungle, trying to find a way to survive.

Is that life, is that what was intended for mankind? The love radiated within me, and I could see clearly what was intended for man, love, light and energy, everyone as equals, love and help thy neighbour, achieve what you desire and feel at one with man, what would the world look like if the commandments read more like.

- Gods have been known in many forms. To have belief and faith in love and the greater good is all you need.
- Idols give you the passion to aspire to do more and achieve your personal life's goal.
- Your God, however you depict them will always stand by your side through the good and the bad. It

will hear your cries and aid to assist you always. So, cry out their names.

- Remember the day which is sacred to you and celebrate it with love and light.
- You will face life's challenges with honour and courage, accept every man or woman as an equal.
- You shall listen to your heart and follow its path.
- You shall not go hungry.
- You shall love your neighbour.
- You shall achieve what you desire, with love, dignity, and pride.

Maybe if the commandments looked more like this, man wouldn't feel so much like a failure, he wouldn't try to trample on another man, disrespect another man's point of view, trash another man's business or name to advance his own career, man wouldn't just think of himself alone. Man wouldn't be in fight or flight mode, man would be at peace, man would feel unconditional love, how would man survive then?

Could that even be possible for earth or mankind? Mankind is polluted, with hate, jealousy, envy, mistrust, and possessiveness, that even they cannot see what they are doing. This isn't the fault of mankind, man has now been indoctrinated to believe this is the way. One person's interpretation, to create fear and control mankind. Adam and Eve were portrayed to have sinned by eating the apple, but have you ever thought, they had just been born and they were 'really' hungry, so they ate what was available, why is that a sin? It states that they were told not to eat anything from the garden, but who told you that? Did Adam or Eve? Did your God?

I think the answer is no, it was one man's depiction and was aimed to control people's minds, do as I say or else, and that is the way the world works, people constantly saying do as I say. Those threatening words. Do as I say, or you will have no job. Do as I say, or you will go back to the children's home. Do as I say would ring true in every man's mind, he would not stand his ground, as fear of the repercussions were too great.

Man is tainted. So, how does it help me being here, in my stunning energy field, feeling all happy and positive when the fate of man is on earth. Ah, that's why I went back, that's why returned, mankind is coming to an end, man will destroy man, but what can I do?

How can I possibly help? I am only a child on earth, without the wisdom of my years, I remember nothing on earth and only bits whilst I am here. So, how did I possibly think that I could save mankind, a 14-year-old lass with mental health issues, who chose to be born to a farming family thought she could save mankind? Flipping heck, what was I thinking, obviously I wasn't thinking, otherwise I would have birthed myself in a family of influence and politics, but it all happened so quick, so how was I going to remember the original plan?

Chapter 3

Suddenly, I was back in body, viciously shaking. Was I having a seizure? I had seen this on TV where someone has a seizure, swallows their tongue, then poof, they are gone, well maybe not so quickly, so I just relaxed until the shaking had stopped, but it didn't. I was scared to open my eyes, one minute I was in an idyllic forest, feeling happy and relaxed, and now what? I could hear their screams.

"What the hell was she doing?" Nessa screamed.

Arty said, "I don't know, she's a freak, she doesn't belong here."

The shaking and the smacks continued until I opened my eyes. Horror struck as they all looked over me, "What's wrong? What have I done? I was asleep."

"No, you weren't asleep, you were talking to someone."

"You're a freak, why the hell are you here, what the hell are you? Her words were filled with venom, she really didn't need to hit anyone, her words could cut you worse than any punch or smack. Nessa with a face of Angel."

With my eyes wide open, I could see into her soul, and it was barely lit; darkness was consuming her, and she was unable to see it, her anger, her hate was eating her alive, and as soon as her soul darkens, there is no way to relight the flame. My eyes softened as I looked at her, and she looked away; she couldn't even look at me, her hatred was buried deep within, unable to see good in anything or anyone. Nessa was full of self-loath, she not only hated me, but she hated herself, that's why she sought vengeance on a vulnerable child, blame something else, its far easier than accepting blame for yourself.

"I am sorry," I said, with the warmth of all my heart, in the hope that it would be accepted. Jay had stepped in and looked at me with kind eyes; for once, there was light in his eyes, I let my eyes do the talking as they thanked him for his understanding, Arty scowled his pig like eyes darted looking everyway but at mine. His jealousy and envy were emitting he was seeing an opportunity, how would he twist this to meet his needs? Nessa had stopped shaking me, she had gone, probably to tell mother that I was sleep talking.

Really, is that such a big thing? Children do it all the time, they have imaginary friends and people who they confide in within their own minds, so what is wrong with that. Nessa will make such a big thing of this, to deflect what is going on within herself, she knows that I know. I have seen her popping those pills which make her go to the toilet, those pills which she believes make her pretty.

When Nessa was younger, she was beautiful, full of life and energy, fantastic athletic figure, muscular and toned, but now her skin hung on her bones, she had no muscle, no bottom, and no boobs. Nessa had lost that much weight and she thought she needed to lose more; it was as if the darkness was consuming her from within, goading her to submit to its wishes. I don't know where Nessa's pain came from, but she wasn't going to continue hurting me, I wasn't going to allow it. Nessa was ill, and if somebody didn't say something, then she would certainly die. Her light was fading, this is what I could see, maybe it's a gift I brought back from Havenmoor?

Was Havenmoor even real, or was it just a dream? It must have been one hell of a dream if I was talking in my sleep. Had they heard my conversation with the light workers? Had they heard my spiel? Or, even worse had they heard my thoughts, did I communicate my thoughts, did I tell them that I constantly wished I wasn't here? I didn't allow my negative self-doubt to get the better of me this time; instead I welcomed it as an old friend, I greeted it with love and compassion and warmed to its embrace, instead of keeping its hold, it suddenly let go of me and I was free, and I felt good.

In fact, I felt better than good; normally, I would fear the outcomes or the wrath of my siblings, I would fear the repercussions. But, for once in my sorry life, I could see them for who they truly are, sad souls, merely existing in life because they don't have the will to live their truth. They don't have the will to love and accept, they can only feel hurt, darkness and hate, but this isn't the way, is it?

I know I have always felt different, I look different and 'definitely' act different than all my family, yet they are my family, they are the people who have raised me, and I suppose I am no different to them, as I felt hurt and dislike towards them too. I can't ever remember feeling any love towards my mother, as I looked at her as the punisher. The one I had to stay away from the one who hurt me with her words which stung worse than a scorpion's sting, but was this because she was also hurting? Why did she fear my father's return so much? Why did this make her so sad? She should have been happy that her husband was home to help her and assist in the farming chores, this was not how it was meant to be.

I was so blinded by my own thoughts and feelings, I never stopped to think of those around me. I was selfish and inconsiderate, I see that now, I thought that it was them who were hurting me. They punished me for being a child, yet they didn't have to because I punished myself enough and blamed them, just as they are blaming me for how they feel. I constantly wished for it all to end, I constantly wished that I wasn't alive. I constantly wished my family weren't my family, maybe I should have just accepted what is, then my life would have been easier. I had been doing exactly what they are doing, why didn't I see it sooner, why didn't I see their hurt and pain?

We cloak our pain by whatever needs necessary, we make certain the world cannot see it, we wear makeup to mask our true features, we wear nice clothes to mask our bodily features, and why? Because this is who the world wants us to be, this is the world's stage, and we must conform. The media portrays pictures of beautiful women making us feel that this is how we must look, thin women with no feminine trait, no natural curves, flat stomachs, and manmade boobs which look like they have been plonked on the chest, their faces look tight with big lips which look like they've been pumped up, brows that don't move and perfect skin which just doesn't look natural.

This portrayal is untrue, yet it is a portrayal that every woman wishes to conform to and will do anything to achieve it. Yet this is fake. Hiding their true selves through products and surgery, is this who we have become? Man trying to make man look better, but these are only the vessels, the real man is inside, barely breathing barely alive, as their souls are unable to live their life's goal. Their souls are struggling under the pressure, their lights are dimming, and soon dark energies will take over, and the light will have lost another soul, Havenmoor will have lost another soul.

Glimpses of Havenmoor flickered in my mind. I can feel their energy, I can feel their presence, their gentle touch guiding me, keeping on the path. I can't believe how clear I can see, and how the world looks so different, I feel like I have woken up from a very long sleep and am now able to live life the way I intended. I'm not quite certain that what I dreamt was real, but it certainly felt real, and even if it wasn't real, it gave me hope, hope of a better future or even of a better end. I suppose in some way, it gave me something to look forward to, if one day I could ascend how great would that be, this is my last lifetime and I'm gona make the most of it.

Caught up in my own thoughts, I didn't notice Fin come into the Kitchen.

"Now then, what have you been up to?" He asked with a little smirk, his dimple was deeper than normal. As I turned, I could feel his energy, and then wow, his energy field was pastel blue, it looked as clear as a Caribbean Ocean, well the pictures I've seen anyway, it shone so bright, and encased his being. Taken back a bit, I smiled and said, "I don't know what you're talking about."

"You absolutely freaked them out, they are all panicking, saying you're a witch, and all sorts, you had better watch yourself." I turned and looked at him inquisitively, "I can't quite understand why such a panic, just because someone talked in their sleep, people do it all the time."

"Yeh, they do, Molly, but they don't turn blue and rise of the bed, that's what they said you did."

"Don't be so stupid." I scoffed. "How the hell could I do that?"

"Obviously, Arty has been on the magic mushrooms again or been taking some of that funny powder with his mates. Nessa is malnourished and hallucinating and well, Jay…" I had nothing to say about Jay, because even though he was spoilt he did have a good heart, he was just easily led and easily manipulated. "Did Jay see too?" Fin looked like he was deep in thought, before he answered with a giggle, "It was just Nessa who saw it and she called to Jay and Arty, they were closest, I don't know how you're gona get out of this one." He gave me a gentle pat on the shoulder, shrugged his shoulders then he was gone.

I stood and pondered for a while, what's the worst that can happen? They can kill me; well, we all know how I would feel about that, I would most definitely welcome it, or they could make my life more miserable than I can ever imagine, or they could just leave me alone and let me crack on. I shuddered to think of what they would do, then a peaceful feeling waved over my body, calming me from the inside out. They can do no more to me than what I allow them to do. I am in control and I am the one who chooses what persecution I require. Feeling rather smug with myself for the decision I had made, I decided this was the way forward. I, myself in control of my own thoughts and emotions, it was no one else's power, just my own.

Havenmoor, it must have been real, how amazing is that? Havenmoor is an actual place where our souls born from, and I am a very old soul, well I am an elder soul, so does that mean that I am the wise? My mind went back to my family of light and my people, their radiant colours, and their peaceful essence, I was back where I belong, I could hear them talking to me. I calmed my mind and asked for one at a time, as I stood there, I was no longer a 14-year-old child, I felt like the master. The master who had awakened from a very long sleep, a master who was going to save his people. Is this why I came back to the earth? Is this why I am here?

Captivated in the recollection of my journey, I was interrupted by Arty, as he pushed past me to get the milk out of the fridge. I could feel his energy and knew instantly what his intention was, so I stepped out of the way, so as he could not intensify the situation, his beady eyes darted bad energy my way, but this time, I could feel the protective barrier repel the darkness and I just smiled.

How was he even alive? The darkness had absorbed him, he was lost in spite and guile, always trying for others to like him, and they did, he could win anyone over. Arty had the touch of an angel when it came to manipulation and winning people over, he was so convincing. His kind words of concern, his attention to the subject and the interest he showed was credible, as he reeled them in hooking their trust. Then when Arty chose, he would dispose of them, stab them in the back and act like nothing had ever happened, he could lie and stare you in the face when doing so, my god he was good.

Arty was an unnatural force, his energy was so dark that I couldn't see it, but weird enough, I could feel it. He didn't say anything, which was a little strange as Arty always had something to say, his devious mind worked in mysterious ways. Arty was the nemesis I needed to defeat, as his poison would cut deep in this family, turning them against each other and themselves. Maybe this is my journey, maybe I need to conquer Arty first, before moving onto the rest of the world, ha ha.

Arty will be no easy feat, his controlling demeanour will be difficult to break, and even harder to get others to see what he 'actually' does, the way he gets them to do exactly what he wants them to do, without them even noticing. Arty would make an excellent politician, but something tells me he hasn't got the balls to go up against someone who has real power; he just loves to pray on the vulnerable and the weak, he's a taker of light, then when he's taken the light and broken them, he moves onto the next tired soul.

We all know people like this in our lives, we all know people who drain our energy. You may not think about it when you are with them, but when you have stepped away from them your head will pound. It's like having an elastic band wrapped around your temples, it will throb with a dull pain, as your energy struggles to replenish, then when you are surrounded with love, you will feel better again. The people I am talking about are light takers, they absorb the light, they take it until it is no more, then they use the light for darkness, turning more souls, and controlling those souls to do their bidding, thus the negative, dark energy of the world.

The world cannot survive on dark energy alone, it needs a balance. There has always been light and dark, there has always been good and evil, but now the evil is escalating, knocking the earth out of kilt, making it unbalanced, thus making it unstable. The earth needs to stabilise if it is going to survive, the balance needs to return. The first step to returning this balance is to understand it, and deal with what is at hand, family. If I can save the family in which I was born, then I can do the same for the rest of mankind, how hard can it be? I've got love on my side, and love always prevails, doesn't it?

Well, that has yet to be proven, but I will have a go. Arty just stood and watched me as I scooped my porridge out of the pan, I didn't rise to him, I just kept smiling. I knew who I was, I knew where I had come from, but he didn't, he didn't know who he was. He wasn't aware that the darkness had taken him, he probably didn't even realise, so he was who he was, and accepting that seemed to come easy to him, he was comfortable being the way he was.

The porridge was gloopy as I scooped it out, it stuck to the spoon, I shook it a little to encourage it to release, it slid and fell into the bowl with a plop. I got the milk out of the fridge and poured it into the bowl, so as the porridge would thin a little. All the time I was preparing my breakfast, Arty stood and watched me, just waiting for the right moment to pounce, just waiting for the right moment to cause trouble, but I didn't give him the satisfaction. I got my porridge and went outside with the bowl.

What a bloody mistake. Mother really didn't like us taking table ware outside as it rarely came back in, so Arty shouted, "Molly has taken her bowl outside." Mother came to the door and shouted me in, as I got to the door, before she could raise her hand, I said, "I'm sorry, mother, I just wanted to get out of the kitchen." No sooner had I said it then her face softened with an accepting nod. Phew that was a first, no smack, no reprimand, no screaming for what occurred last night, was this the future, they all feared me?

Back into the kitchen I went, Arty stood there sneering, making him look uglier than he already did. I just smiled and in walked mother behind me. "I can't believe you let her get away with that. She went outside with a bowl, she knows we are not allowed to do that, she knows." Mother just looked at him and said, "Oh, Arty, give it a break, stop causing trouble." Arty couldn't believe what he was hearing as he looked dumbfounded and stormed out of the kitchen.

I looked over to mother in a thankful manner, and appreciated her not smacking me; in fact, she felt different. Mother normally felt tired and irritable, but today she felt lighter, her energy was lifted. I looked at her closely and still couldn't see her energy field; in man's words, it's called an Aura, but for me its energy; mothers' energy hadn't yet gone, she must have fought like mad to keep it glowing. There was a glimmer of hope for her yet. Feeling reassured, I finished my breakfast, then went outside to find Fin.

Chapter 4

I couldn't quite believe that I averted punishment this morning, that would normally have escalated into something huge, yet it didn't, why? Was it because I was 'actually' aware, or was it because they think I'm a witch and can cast a spell on them? I can't quite fathom what is happening, they were all freaking out this morning, yet no one has mentioned it, no one has even called me. Oh wait, I have yet to see Nessa, she will be the one, she will be the one who calls me a freak, and weird, but for now I'm just going to enjoy the peace and quiet.

I headed outside, it was a beautiful day, the sun was still low in the sky, rising from the east and casting shadows over the lush green lawn. This lawn was my mothers' pride and joy, she scrabbled to keep the chickens off it, as they dug up her magnificent roses. Mother loved her flowers, and had roses of all kinds, the apricot roses were my favourite and guess what they were called? 'Molly,' they were a hybrid tea rose and their scent was intoxicating. Sometimes, mother let me help her prune her roses back, or weed the borders; in the past, I saw this as a chore, or a punishment, but now I feel blessed that she shared her love of gardening with me, as this was my love too.

Maybe I had been looking at mine and my mother's relationship wrong, always expecting the punishment, always expecting the smack. Maybe my expectations are what attracted it, maybe if I didn't think about it, or fear it so much, maybe just maybe it wouldn't happen? Who am I trying to kid? Of course, it's going to happen. *Molly you cannot be that naïve*, but if what I am thinking is correct then there could be a chance that I can change the relationship with my mother, and instead of fearing her, and somewhat really disliking her, maybe I could show a little love and compassion?

I could feel my heart soften, because where would I be without my mother, obviously I wouldn't have been born, or I would have been born but into another family. Would another family have given me as much colour and variety as this one? Would another family have challenged me the way that this one has? I have always wished for things to be easier, if only I didn't have this family, or if only I had lots of money, or if only I wasn't alive. So, what have I been doing, why have I wasted 14 years of my life wishing for things be different? Why can't I just embrace what is and enjoy it like I intended to?

I really cannot answer the questions above, but I do know that my life was tainted from the day I entered the earth. My mother apparently wanted more children, then had me and was unable to have any more children. I think that this is a good thing, both for her and the children, but this meant that we never 'bonded' and my mother blamed me, a baby, I had no choice, no control, yet she blamed me and was angry. It's so easy to blame others for what we know wasn't their fault, for something that they can't possibly control, yet this is what happened, I can see that now, my mother blamed me for being born.

As the thoughts flowed through my mind, I reflected on all the times me and mother had spent any time together, the times when I didn't feel like she despised me, the times I 'actually' felt close to her. The times were rare, but they had been there, I just didn't notice, because I had filled my head with all the horrible things my mother had done and said to me, I had forgotten all the times, when she had been nice and even loving.

My heart felt like it was breaking, the pain hurt more now than it did when I felt anger, hurt and distrust, at least before it was a dull ache, but now, it feels like its breaking in two, all the missed times. All the missed opportunities. I knew I had to mend this rift between us, because mothers are precious, despite their actions and I had a feeling that my mother wouldn't be here for much longer.

As I thought, I walked in search of my brother Fin; I let my mind meander in positive consideration to ease my broken heart.

I soon found Fin and sure enough, he was in the pen with his calves; his calves were his pride and joy, they were Aberdeen angus calves which had been abandoned by their mothers. Fin had hand-reared them with powder milk and a lot of love. The calves were extremely cute, jet black with pink noses, they were gentle animals and always loved a hug, like extra-large teddy bears. Fin loved his animals, all sorts of animals, cows, pigs, chickens, and ducks.

If he weren't rearing the animals to sell, he would be rearing them to show. He had reared chickens from all over the world; they were mighty fine and well taken care of, their feathers glistened, their claws and toes were clean and bright; in fact, their beds were cleaner than the hall floor in the house. Fin had great pride in his animals, and I loved sharing the experience with him, as he allowed me to help him care for them. We always said that one day we would buy our own farm together; I honestly could not think of anything which would make me happier.

Fin smirked as I helped and soon said, "So, how is it going? Have you had an ear bashing yet? Have you come here to get out of the way?"

Fin was always my go-to man, he made me laugh and forget about my woes, as I knew I wasn't alone. Fin got his share of hidings too, he often felt mother's wrath, or father's taunts, so chose to spend time with those he loved, and those who loved him, his animals. Fin cared for his animals, he was attentive and kind, his animals were always clean and never wanted for anything, as Fin would pay for everything himself. Fin was quite a wealthy young man, as the animals he reared, he sold at market, helping to contribute to the running of the house and mother. However, when father became aware of this, he would also expect his cut. Thus, the reason why father was never told, what he didn't know didn't hurt.

Father would take anything, he would always make you feel like he is doing you a favour, but he wasn't. He loathed the fact that his own son was more successful than he was, so he goaded Fin with his hurtful words.

Well? He said, "What has been said?"

I looked at him and replied, not quite believing the words which were coming from my voice. "Nothing, Arty has been his usual self, you know trying to make trouble, but hasn't said anything about the incident."

He starred back with a baffled look, then out of the blue asked "Do you ever feel like you don't belong here?" "Sometimes I feel like I was born at the wrong time. Or maybe to the wrong family." I replied with reluctancy, as I felt way worse than what I had communicated.

"Yeh, I get that. I would love to see my birth certificate and see who my actual parents are. Or maybe we were swapped at birth and have been given to the wrong family." He chortled as he said it, and that dimple reappeared on his cheek.

"What actually happened last night?" He asked with a look of genuine concern.

"Honestly, I was having a vivid dream, and was in a tranquil meadow, then all these colours came from a forest, and surrounded me, they said I was as old as time, and that I have been born to the earth for a reason."

"They were right about that, you were born to annoy me," laughter shone in his face as he spoke the words, I knew he was teasing, so paid him no attention as I smirked in reply, but then he softened and asked with sincerity.

"So, what was the reason?" I wasn't 'actually' sure whether he was interested or if he was taking the Michael, but he seemed authentic. "I don't know what the reason was, we didn't get to that point, as I was awoken with a vicious shake." Nervous laughter arose in me, as if I was trying to cover something up, but I couldn't, as I knew I feared Nessa, and her venom, and Fin knew this too.

He sniggered again and said, "Ah, that's a shame, it would have been nice to know, that you weren't just sent here to bug me." I laughed at his silly reply. "Do you actually believe I went to that place; do you actually believe in the soul and spirituality?"

"Do you really have to ask?" He replied, again with his little smirk. I could see his energy dancing as it glowed, he emanated power and love, his beautiful calming nature was a pleasure to be around. No wonder, his animals loved him so much; animals are great judges of character, and with that thought, Fin exclaimed.

"Come on, if you're going to help me, you can brush that calve, it's going to market later, and we need her to look her best."

I got the brush out of the tatty box on the pen floor, it was a soft bristle brush, which made the calves coat shine when you stroked it along her back, you always went with the flow of the coat, not unlike brushing your own hair. Dorris looked like she was enjoying her pamper and Fin finished mucking out around us. Fin was fast at scooping that dung, and it didn't take long, until he was laying a full new bed of straw, as it kept the calves coat shiny, and he didn't want her going to market dirty.

"What time are you going to market?" I asked.

"10 o' clock. Hague is picking up the calves and transporting them for me." Hague is a farmer from the next village; he spent a lot of time with Fin, as father was always at work delivering bread. Hague was kind and gentle, he taught Fin how to identify the traits of a healthy calve, how to rear, them and feed them, so as they would make good money when they were sold for beef stock or breeding in the future. Fin was only 14, nearly 15 and obviously couldn't drive, and neither could mother, so Hague would pick up and collect the cattle so as Fin didn't have to ask father to have any time off work, as he knew that Fin would not ask.

"Are you going to market?" I asked in a hopeful manner; if he was going to market then I would make myself scarce, Immy isn't here, so I would have no one, which made my 14-year-old self a little apprehensive.

"No, I'm not going to market today, Hague is taking another farmer, so there is no room, I'm here for the duration," he said wirily.

The time soon came, and Hague reversed down the drive and to the farm gate; I helped Fin to build makeshift fences so as the calves could walk out of the pen and into the wagon. This was no easy quest, as the farm was small and didn't have many spare gates lying around, but we gathered what we could.

Hague came to see what we were doing as we lowered the ramp on the cattle wagon. The cattle wagon was a huge silver wagon with a bright burgundy flash blazed across it. Hague smiled as he saw us both scurrying to make the fences.

"Good morning, young Molly, how are you today?" His energy radiated from him, drawing me in to his warmth.

"I'm good, thank you." I replied with a thankful heart.

Hague returned my smile a hundred-fold, it looked like his entire body was smiling and his energy field was red. I've never seen a red energy field before, and many would think that red would mean danger, but I knew that couldn't be true as Hague's vibration is one of good, he has a strong connection with nature, the physical body and the material world; he is extremely well balanced and seems to know what he wants from this world. Hague is a soul which manifests his desires and makes them so; he is passionate and unapologetic about his life experiences, sharing them with those who would listen. Hague is a powerful being who has a lust for life, he is unafraid of anything. It's very easy to bask in his energy.

"Hoy, are you helping, or just standing there daydreaming?" Fin giggled as Hague had shouted over, awakening my trance like stand, one blink of the eyes and I was back. I giggled back and looked at Fin absently. "Where are all the tatty gates?"

"A fairy came and got rid of them while you were asleep, and replaced them with shiny new ones," laughing as he said it, then winking at Fin.

"Ah, ah, I'm not that dumb, I presume you had them in your wagon." Hague was forever prepared, as the sheep hurdles were most definitely new, or very well taken care of. The hurdles are like individual gates which interlock, making it very easy to lengthen into a fence; they are about 5ft long, 2.5ft high and manageable, making the whole job of loading calves a lot easier. Fin loaded the calves, he walked behind them waving his arms about and telling them to get on, whilst I stood by the fence shooing any calve which came my way.

They were soon loaded, and Fin closes the back gates of the wagon to keep them safe. We all work together to remove the hurdles and place them in a box under the wagon, where they are cleverly hidden, making more room in the wagon for life stock. The calves are mooing impatiently, they do not seem to like being in a metal box on wheels, but they soon calm once the engine starts.

Hague dusts of his clothes to clean his hands and say his goodbyes, but instead "Are you coming?" He asks Fin. Fin looks at me and says, "No, its OK, I thought you were taking another farmer today."

"No, his wife isn't well, so he's staying home, there's enough room for two, if Molly wants to come." I'm sure Hague knew the reason that Fin didn't want to go was because of me. I didn't need to be asked again, I eagerly jumped in the wagon and off we all went. I was very excited. The wagon was extremely clean, as was its owner. Hague was always very smart, wearing trousers, a shirt and tie, partly covered by a richly made waistcoat, the front was green suede, the back, plush burgundy satin. His boots were immaculate, tan leather with tartan material on the insets near the laces, he exuded the confidence of a fine country gentleman, you would never have guessed he was a farmer, well other than the smell. The smell that no sheep farmer could ever get away from, but I loved.

The seat in the wagon was one long bench, there was no gear knob or handbrake disrupting the elongated value of the smartly covered bench seat. I perched myself right in the middle, with prime view of the road ahead, unlike life itself, sitting between my two favourite men, Fin and Hague was a huge relief, and one I welcomed with all my heart, home was but a distant memory for now. The energy in the wagon was positive and happy, Hague told us about all his adventures, speaking with exhilaration.

Sharing his love of travel whilst increasing his skills in farming, learning from some of the most advanced farmers in the world. His explorations were awe inspiring and made me crave for more information. He took us on adventures in the outback of Australia to the mountainous terrain of New Zealand and the Balkan lands of Eastern Asia. Hague was only 28, he had no children of his own, and his wife ailed with body pain and fever called multiple sclerosis.

There was no cure to this condition; however, Mary dealt with the condition well, using her knowledge of plants and flora, managing the condition in an alternative manner through natural remedies and meditation. There was but one alternative to Mary's way and that was drugs, pain meds which would have dulled her senses and increased her body weight; that was not a risk Mary was willing to take. Thus, she threw herself into a life of not only helping herself but helping others through her experience of the cruel condition which had afflicted her.

Mary was a true beauty, with fair skin and red hair. Her sculptured bone structure defined her face, pale pink cheeks prominent, button nose and earthy green eyes. It was no wonder Hague loved her so much, as all his journeys were shared with his wife by his side. One learning about the healing ways of nature and the other learning how farmers can manage the land in a more sustainable way, beneficial to both man and the planet. His stories were fascinating, taking us on journeys we could only ever dream of Hague made anything possible, nothing was out of reach.

We soon arrived at the cattle market, the market was immense with sheep hurdles dividing the roads, and paths; I don't know how Hague knew where to go, but he drove to the exact gate required, dropped the ramp, and let the cattle amble into their new pen. As Dorris came of last, she gave a lasting look to Fin, who smiled in the knowledge that she would be OK.

Dorris was being sold for breeding, she had a pure bloodline, with great build and structure, resonating pure health, she would bare healthy calves in the future. Fin was confident in his knowledge of calves and other livestock; in fact, he could tell you a million interesting things about caring for them but ask him to write a paragraph and he could not do it. Fin knew he wasn't the sharpest knife in the cutlery draw, but he could hold his own in cattle a market; he knew the prices, he knew the percentage the market would take, and he knew the exact payment to expect when he went into the market office to be paid.

He may not be good with words, but there was nothing wrong with his math, if only his teachers could see him today. Fin's teachers were constantly on his case about the inability to read or write, they even referred us both to a speech therapist, as they knew Fin wouldn't go on his own, therefore I went for moral support, and to learn a little too.

The market began, the cattle pen (this was the pen where they showcased the animals) was made of 6ft metal hurdles, like the small sheep gates Hague has, but bigger. The arena took centre stage in the middle of a large barn which was made of tin and old wood. The farmers stood around in their little packs waiting for the bidding to begin. There was an excited energy in the air, the room was filled with an array of colours, rich yet clear; my senses were heightened as I absorbed this spell binding atmosphere.

Soon, the auctioneer stood on the box at the side of the pen. The auctioneer was a tall slender man, his eyes were bright and kind which lightened his weathered face; he stood tall and proud, sturdy in his stance, ready to do his bidding. As the gaggle went down, the room was silenced and in came the first calve. The bidding started, it was fast, I couldn't keep up to what price they were at, what was for sale, what had been sold, it was all a big blur.

I stood with Fin and Hague; Fin wasn't buying today, he was selling, but Hague was buying, but I didn't see what he bought. In fact, I didn't see him bid. Hague's stature was like royalty, he was extremely well liked, and everyone knew him; his smile could light up a room, and his laugh was infectious.

In came Fin's lot, I could feel his tension, the first six brought good money and Fin was happy with the price; then in came Dorris, she was his pride and joy, the bidding started. I could feel Fin hold his breath, I gently gripped his hand and said, "breathe;" he turned and smiled that cheeky smile and my heart filled. I hoped Dorris would make good money for him.

The bidding never seemed to stop. Dorris was one year old and hit a record high for any young heifer sold in the market, making a staggering £800. The other cattle had brought half that amount, Fin was beaming; his energy was of the scale. Everyone came to shake his hand and tell him what a fine animal he had sold, one man pulled him to one side and told him that he would be willing to buy the cattle straight from the shed in future; Fin just shook his head, and the man's energy darkened. Hague stepped in and whispered in the man's ear when he scuttled of like a rat. It was at that point I saw Hague and Fin's energy combine, it was intertwined and dancing like it was happy, it was captivating.

Fin shouted over, "Aare you ready we are off?" I ran towards him, but then slowed as I remembered what I was running to, I'm running to home. Are we going home? I really didn't want to go home. I wanted to stay with Hague, the guardian, I never wanted this day to end. Fin was waving me over, and I didn't want to anger him. "Come on, we'll go have a bacon butty in the café."

"My treat," Hague said.

I happily trotted alongside them, they were discussing money and the biddings of the day; apparently Hague had bought eight cattle, which we still had to load. The café's aroma was welcoming; bacon, sausage, onions, and mushrooms washed out the smell of farmers, their bodily odour and personal hygiene was somewhat unkept. Hague went to the counter and ordered the butties, the plump lady with the round face was zealous in her serving, as if she couldn't do enough to please Hague. Her eyes darting constant glances at him whilst she was working; in fact, she never took her eyes of him; I would say she has a crush; I giggled a little inside.

Hague came over, and gave us the butties, we both thanked him and tucked into our heavenly sandwich. The butties were made on thick cut white bread, the juice oozed out of them, from the dripping in the bacon fat, they were delicious. As we ate, farmers kept coming to congratulate Fin, so meaningful in their words, one man even said it was a momentous moment, as your price gives us all hope that anything is achievable. It was lovely to hear the praise my brother was receiving, and he deserved it, he worked hard and never ailed or wailed; he was pure good, but sometimes pure good attracts.

I could feel it, the darkness-it was looming, like a serpent waiting to strike, its energy was thick like tar. I could feel it coming closer and closer, wishing for it not to happen, *please don't spoil Fin's day, this is Fin's day*. Fin and Hague were deep in conversation unaware of the feeling I felt. Hague towered over Fin by a good two foot, which settled me as he could shield him. The energy plunged towards them both, as the strange man who had pulled Fin to one side earlier lunged with his fists at Hague. Hague stepped out the way and laughed, which made the man even more angry.

"How can you possibly feel threatened by a child?" He teased. The man's energy was a thick dark red, intertwined with black; it was heavy. I could sense the weight of it, as it forged the man forward again and again, lashing out, was he 'actually' trying to hit Hague, or was he trying to release himself from the energy which surrounded him. The other farmers soon gathered around, trying to see what was happening, but two strapping farmers picked the strange man up by his arms and took him outside.

Chapter 5

The café was buzzing with eager gossip, everyone surmising why the man lunged at Hague, but Hague was having none of it, he stood on a chair and whistled to get everyone's attention. The room stopped and they looked up, his voice was deep and robust. "You all know me, and you know Fin, well that piece of vermin just threatened a 14-year-old boy, and I won't have it; we are a family, a community and we look out for each other." The farmers were jeering and raising their hands in warm gestures.

One farmer shouted out, "Yeh, Fin is our good luck charm, he's just got the best price for a young heifer ever, he gives us hope, no one threatens Fin." Hague put his hands up to calm his fellow farmers. "We need to be here for each other, we cannot have outsiders coming into our markets and threatening the way we do business." More cheers filled the room, the happy, positive energy resumed. We finished our butty and washed it down with a swig of Hague's coffee. Hague and Fin said their goodbyes and off to the wagon we went.

"What about your pay?" I asked Fin.

"Oh, I got it," Hague replied, and handed over the money to Fin. "I didn't want Fin holding that amount of money, I know those guys in there and they are good, but you can never be too careful, that someone isn't going to take advantage." He smiled as he said it, and I smiled back. Fin stood holding the cash, it looked a lot, I said "Put it in your pocket before anyone sees it." Fin quickly placed the cash in his pocket, and we jumped in the wagon, "Wait what about your calves?" I said, and then heard the rustling in the back of the wagon.

"I got some young farm hands to load them for me, they need the pocket money."

"Oh," I replied, then settled into my seat. Fin was happy, he had a great day, and achieved so much; it's a shame that his own family can't see his success, it's a shame that when he gets home, he won't be able to speak of this day, and 'definitely not' speak of the success he has had, otherwise we all know what happens then.

"Who was that guy?" Fin finally spoke up.

"I don't know who he was, I could see him bothering you, and just asked him to leave politely, or else," he smirked as he said it. "I've never seen him in the market before, I don't know him, but I felt like I did know him if that makes sense, he had some familiarity about him." Fin looked deep in thought, when his face brightened and shouted out, "I know who he reminded me of!"

"Who?"

"Father! Those bright blue weasel eyes, that hook nose, the mottled skin on the neck which looked like a turkey neck."

The man was plumper than father, but was definitely the same height, his face was more rounded, making his hook nose look out of place, but yes, I could see the resemblance, and that energy, eeek yes, maybe Fin is right.

"Mmmmm I can see where you're coming from Fin, but we know father's brothers-there's only two, Ken and Bert."

"No, he has a third brother, called Jimmy, we haven't met him before as he has lived away, but I've heard father talking on the phone to a Jimmy."

"Well, why would father's brother threaten you? Shouldn't family be proud of other family members' achievements? Hague just made the entire farming community our family, they have more pride and appreciation than our own family do." So, 'really,' I just answered my own question, are family ever truly proud of their siblings, parents, children, or any other family member, or is jealousy just that in any form, not distinguishing from family, friends, or foes?

The silence was deafening, when Fin spoke out, "Maybe he wasn't threatening me, maybe it was just a request." Hague shot him a sharp glance. "That was no request, lad, that was a definite threat, it wasn't the words he used, more the white hand print he left on your arm, because of his grip."

"I know you are just trying to make sense of it, but I'm certain, it will all work out, the other farmers will watch out for you too, so I don't think he will be back in that market any time soon."

Fin seemed to ease a little, but I could tell he was worried, his mind was working overtime. I leant over and gave him a little nudge with my shoulder. "It will be OK, as long as we have each other, it will be OK." I got a slight grin out of him, but no dimple, so I knew he was worried.

The journey home seemed to take no time at all; the journey there took at least an hour, the journey back was 40 minutes tops. We turned down our lane, which seemed darker than normal, the branches were hanging low over the lane, breaking off as the wagon hit them one by one, I don't remember them being that low when we went, but now it feels eerie.

As we pulled up at the end of the drive, Hague asked. "Whose is that car?" We stopped our decent and looked. "Its father's," I said. Then Fin seemed to freeze, his body rigid and unable to move. "What is he do,oo,oo,ing back so early, he doesn't normally finish till dark, and we are ready for bed, why is he home?" Fin stuttered, his mouth moving more than his body was.

Hague looked worriedly at Fin, "Are you OK, lad? Its only your father." But Hague knew that look on Fin's face, one of dread and despair, he knew because he had seen it before.

Fin looked at Hague replying. "Yeh, I know its only father, its OK, I'm just shocked because he isn't usually home this early, it's just weird that's all."

"Do you want me to come in with you? We can tell them the good news about the selling price of your, cattle , they will be extremely proud of you, I know I am."

"God no, we can't tell them what Fin has made, they will take it off him, he will be made to give it to them."

"Don't be silly, lass, your parents won't make Fin do that. Will they Fin? They are good folk." Fin just looked absently at Hague with nothing to say. Hague was a good man, and had helped Fin for the past two years, he had been introduced to Fin by a schoolteacher who was a farmer, he knew Fin's interest, but also had suspicions of the family situation, so he asked if Hague would help with the transport. Mr Fenton was an extremely understanding teacher who understood vocational studies, he even gave Fin Thursday mornings off to go to market. How many teachers would do that?

As we jumped out the wagon, father stepped out the back door, his face was bright red, his eyes were intense which sent a bitter chill down my spine. This man whom we called father was a bully, not a confrontational bully, but a mind games bully. He was always putting Fin down, nothing was ever good enough, a bit like the way mother is with me, that's father to Fin.

I could see that Fin was willing for Hague to go before father reached us, but he didn't; he just sat and watched this small, framed man, who was no more than nine stone wet through. Fin turned and waved goodbye to Hague, but he didn't leave; he was intent on seeing father, but father is too clever to leave a handprint, or say a nasty word in front of anyone. We could tell how angry he was, but he hid it well, he always did. He walked straight up to the driver's door, opened it and said thank you to Hague, he really was that good. Now, I see where Arty gets it from.

Hague bowed his head, father slammed the door shut and Hague waved goodbye to us, we both waved back, holding each other's gaze, knowing what was to come. We both tried to act as normal as possible, as if nothing had happened, which it hadn't, so what was there to be worried about? Yet, we were anxious, as we turned, I could see father, his energy field was a wispy dark smoke, I've never seen an energy field like it, the smog that surrounded him, blanked everything else out, there was no background, just a thick choking fog.

"Molly, you can go in and get your tea," he barked over. I just stood there, not wanting to leave my brother's side, but I knew I would be made to. I wanted to protect Fin. I knew what father's plan was, you could see it in his face, you could see the spite eating at him. Fin quickly slipped me the money out of his pocket and whispered, "Hide it." I ran into the house, through the hall and upstairs; I knew exactly where to put it, somewhere that no one would dare go, the airing cupboard in our bedroom.

The house was quite still other than a rustling in the kitchen, they would all still be at work, it was only 4.30. I went up the stairs with speed and headed straight for the airing cupboard. I was right, there was no one home, the room was stagnant and damp, smelling of rotten wood, you could see the rotting wood through the frayed carpet. I opened the airing cupboard with a sharp tug, as sometimes it got stuck, and made a crunchy noise when it opened, so to limit the noise, I was quick.

I went onto my hands and knees and crawled to the corner of the cupboard, this point was in the eaves of the roof and was lower than the rest. In the corner was a heavy dark wooden box which Bell had given me to store all my sewing equipment in, I kept it in the corner as it was as dark as the box, making it difficult to see, and in the hope that my sewing equipment would be left alone. I quickly opened the box and lifted the middle layer, then put the cash in the bottom, trying to cover it up with my bobbins of cotton and needle packets, but it kept bouncing back up, there wasn't enough weight. I pressed it down with my fingers and swiftly put the thin layer over the top, it clicked into place, securing the money, I hastily closed it up, hooking the latch over and locking it tight with a matchstick.

Hearing the commotion downstairs, I was uncertain what to do, do I go down and get the wrath of both, 'or' I could just stay here, I could hear Fin's muffled voice, as he was trying to speak. When Fin was anxious, he would develop a stammer, unable to get his words out, he would just end up throwing his arms up in dismay and lashing out in pure frustration. I could hear father's high-pitched squeal, as he threw a tantrum like a child. "He's made a fool of me in that market, I will never be able to show my face again. I don't know why that man comes to take him, he needs to keep his nose out of our business."

"Has he told you how much he made today? Over £2,000! That's more than I make in a week!"

"Who the hell does he think he is, well, he isn't having that money, I am. He uses my land, my water and electric, that money should be mine." I couldn't hear mother, I don't know who he was shouting at, but what he is saying is true to an extent, Fin does use his water, electric and land, but he also pays mother £50 per week for board, unlike father who gives her £45 per week to raise seven children. Does he even know the extent of what Fin does for this family? Fin doesn't only raise and care for his own animals, he tends the family animals too, the animals mother has bought, but doesn't have enough time in the day to care for, Fin and Erbie are the ones who tends to them, they do all the work.

Father has never bent his back a day in his life. He is only good for taking handouts of the government, crying poverty, stealing, and taking anything anyone else has got. Sad to say that my own father doesn't even realise what he has got. His only good memories are of when he was a child, and how he was close to his father; his father did everything for him, bought him new cars and shared his time with him. They were the happiest times of our father's life, as he constantly tells us; we don't even know why he wanted to have children, as he didn't care for us. He was too selfish and self-absorbed to care for another. I could feel my anger bubbling, my rage my hurt and pain, as my brother was being bullied by his own father.

Father never lifts a finger, it's always Fin, Erbie and mother, they do everything. Father doesn't even help mother to buy or sell the animals, mother has an old family friend called Little Robbie; he buys all her pigs and cattle, and sells them. So, why father believes he deserves anything, I do not know. He is just a spoilt child, throwing his toys out of the pram, wanting attention and anything else he can take. I felt enraged inside, I wanted to scream, to tell him what I thought, to tell him that he is selfish and mean, but I didn't, I just sat in the airing cupboard listening.

The airing cupboard was above the kitchen, there was no insulation, so it was easy, and no one would suspect, as no one dared go into this cupboard. Crouched in the corner, I made myself comfy ready for the long haul; I don't think there's going to be any tea tonight, although I could hear pots and pans clanging in the kitchen. The raised voices had ceased and replaced with whispered murmurs, who was he talking to? I wished I had x-ray vision, and could look through walls, then I wouldn't have to wonder?

Suddenly. "What are you doing here, what rock did you climb under from?" I heard the snigger, then recognised the voice, as he replied "Now, now, Maggie, no need to be like that, it's no way to treat family." There was another giggle which I also recognised, Arty!

It was mother talking to that man, it must be father's brother Jimmy, that's why they were whispering, and Arty what did he have to do with this? Why was he home? It must be past 5 pm, how long had I been up here? But where was Fin, I hadn't heard him for a while.

"Get the hell out of this house, you're not welcome here." Mother's voice hollered, then silence, no noise at all, my ears strained to hear the words, or anything, but nothing, until. Click, the bedroom door latch lifted, that latch was indistinguishable. I froze, the whispered voices were coming closer. They must be looking for the money, I've heard mother and father argue about a Jimmy in the past, their arguments always involved father giving, lending Jimmy money, so I guess this Jimmy isn't a good guy.

I felt as though I was barely breathing, not one noise did I make, I could hear them all looking in the bedroom, there weren't that many places I could hide, three beds, 1 wardrobe and a chest of drawers, what was I going to do hide in a drawer? The door flung open to the airing cupboard, I could feel my body calm as it did so, they were looking right at me, but for some bizarre reason, they couldn't see me. My body was pulsing, fear running through every vein, yet sedated by calmness, how could this be?

Yes, my prayers had been answered I had a superpower of invisibility, or so I thought. The cupboard doors shut, and their voices returned, father, Jimmy, and Arty.

"Well, where is she?"

"I don't know where she is, or where she can be, she's a freak; last night she elevated of the bed and glowed blue, that's how freaky she is."

"What are you talking about, Arty, why am I only hearing of this now?" I could hear father's voice.

"Well, it did only happen last night, and you're not about much, to be honest, you don't know anything that goes on in this house, you haven't got a clue, what I have to put up with." Arty scorned as he made it all about himself as usual.

I couldn't believe what I was hearing, but then again of course, I could believe what Arty was saying, because it always had to be about him. Arty always wanted the limelight, but never got it, as Jay would get it every single piece, even the dog got more attention that Arty. For some reason, mother never took him on, she always kept him at arm's length, and maybe, there was a reason for that, maybe mother sensed the darkness which beholds him.

I wonder why they couldn't see me; I was right there; they were looking straight at me. The calm energy within me was replaced by fear, as it consumed me, my body began to shake uncontrollably, I just needed to stay here until Immy came home, then I would be safe, she would protect me. Immy had left for work earlier than normal this morning, I hadn't seen her all day, I hope she is coming home, what if she didn't, what if she went straight to her boyfriends, what would I do?

I could hear the raised voices downstairs, as Jimmy interrogated mother. "Where is she, are you hiding her? She can't hide forever."

So, now what? Did he want the money, or did he want me? What was the end game? I could hear my mother stand up to him, I had never heard her do this to anyone before, she has a harsh tongue, but she's normally the submissive with father, not the dominant one, that's normally father's role in this relationship, but mother was cutting strips of Jimmy with her tongue, this I was quite accustomed to, as it was normally me, she projected her venom on. Today, mother truly outdid herself, no holding back, she let it all pour out, her spite and abhor for the man she married was cast onto his brother in bucket loads. Phew, I'm 'really' glad I'm not down there.

"Even if I did know where she was, I wouldn't tell you, I've told you before leave this house, you're not wanted here."

Father's voice appeared more desperate, "Just tell him where she is, Maggie, you know he won't leave until he gets what he came for."

"And what's that, Mick (short for Michael)? Money? Why do have to be so spineless, you do nothing for this family but bring humiliation and shame, you are just like him, why don't you both leave, do us a favour."

"Well, it was money, but now I know you have something far greater than money; I believe your daughter has a gift? I believe she can do some out-of-this-world things." Jimmy said with a glare.

Mother laughed uncontrollably, "Who's told you that? Arty? He was hallucinating because of all the drugs he takes. Really, you, trust a drug addict? You will make yourselves a laughing stock if you go around telling people that a kid can turn blue and raise of the bed."

"You already have a son who can outshine you in caring for animals, now you want to break this family by allowing your brother to get his claws into your youngest child?" Mother's tone sounded bitter as she stabbed hurtful remarks to father; she really was going for it, holding no punches, there was strength and honour in her voice, as if she was finally fighting for her life.

The dulcet sound of Arty's voice overpowered all, "I'm not a druggy, no matter what you say, and what I saw is true, just wait until Jay comes home, he will tell you, you are evil, I hate you."

Ouch that must have hurt mother, but she retaliated, "You're the evil one, with your manipulation, you think I don't know what you are like. You think I don't know how you work; Jay tells me everything, you think you are clever, but you're not."

Never in my life had I heard mother speak like that to anyone, especially Arty, so I had read the situation wrong. I thought that they were all in cahoots, I thought they all detested me, I never thought my mother would stand up for me. The warmth overwhelmed my heart again and I could feel it soften even more, my mother did 'actually care' for me and maybe even love me, I have always kept my distance from her, thinking that she was the enemy, but was I wrong?

Their voices had quietened, but I still hadn't heard Fin's voice, where was he, was he OK? I needed to move, but uncertain how I could get down the stairs without them hearing me was a conundrum, until I had a bright idea. I will climb out of the window. This was an upstairs window, which was just above the living room window, to the left of the window was a flat porch roof, which was about 7ft high, so it meant I would need to jump a little, but I'm certain I could do it, after all I was a pretty good gymnast. I pushed open the cupboard door as silently as I could, then tip toed over to the bedroom window.

The wood around the window was discoloured with black and green mould, which was eating into the frame, causing the white paint to flake and fall of. I pushed open the window and climbed onto the ledge; the ledge was slippery as the mould didn't interact well with gloss paint, but I needed to find Fin. I held the window frame to keep my balance then lunged to the right to land onto the porch roof. Feeling quite proud of myself, I went to the edge and lowered myself of the porch roof onto a half barrel planter which was resting against the porch wall.

The barrel was full of soil and weeds, so it was a soft landing. Upon landing, I glanced around quickly to make sure the coast was clear, and I wasn't at risk of being caught. Then there was a flicker of light. I could her the silent hum of a motorbike, well it was a scooter, but Immy called it her bike. I had an idea, if I could get down the drive without being seen, I could get to the bottom of the lane and meet her, tell her what was happening, and maybe, just maybe Immy would save the day.

The coast was clear, I hurried down the side of the parked cars and the trailer which sat idly on the drive, I kept to the hedge so as no one would see me. Once at the end of the drive, I hid in the dense foliage on the corner and waited. The scooter was coming closer and closer; soon it was upon me. I could see a flash of red coming closer, as I stepped out into the lane Immy slammed on her brakes, causing her to wobble a little.

She looked at me in a cursing way, but her face soon relaxed when I smiled. She lifted her face plate whilst trying to talk. "What are you doing, you daft bugger, I could have run into you." I managed another smile until my face turned serious, and I blurted. "Immy, we have a problem. Me and Fin went to market today, Fin made lots of money with his prize cow, and a man came over and threatened him, which we now know to be Uncle Jimmy. Hague stood up to the man, and he didn't seem to like it much, but now he's here and so is father, they want Fin to hand over the money and they think I have got it. I've been hiding for ages, I don't know where Fin is, and I need your help." Wow, all of that without a breath, how the heck?

"Jimmy is here, are you sure its Jimmy, that's not good. Molly, you go to Mrs Farringtons and stay there until I come and get you."

"But what about Fin? I need to find him."

"No, you don't, just leave it to me, I will find Fin, trust me, you need to go to Mrs Farrington." I nodded and left her to park her bike up.

I went own the drive back towards the porch, it was shared drive and Mr. Farrington's cottage was behind our house, but I had to pass the living room window to get there, so down on my knees again and crawled under the window. I could hear them talking but didn't wait around to hear what was being said. Mrs Farrington's front door was about 7ft away from your living room window, so I stayed crouched until I reached her front door.

I knocked on the door and anticipated its opening. Mrs Farrington was an elderly lady, who rarely ever went out, so I knew she would be home. The door opened and I walked in. The cottage was clean and cosy, straight in front of the door were stairs, covered by a heavy tapestry curtain, to the left a low door which went into a living room and to the right it was a door which went into the pantry. The pantry had a table and chairs against the stairs wall, then two armchairs placed Infront of the fire. The fire was made of cast iron and had an oven and a hot plate on it, the kettle was always on and ready to be poured.

Mrs Farrington was a plumpish lady, with hunched shoulders, she rarely smiled and always appeared to be frowning, yet she was kind and caring and had a warmth about her that was trustworthy. Mrs F was always there for mother and me. I followed her into the pantry and there sat on the chair at the side of the fire was Fin, feeling a sense of relief I went over and gave him a big hug. "Thank God, you're OK."

"Yep, mother distracted father enough and gave me time to get here. We all know father doesn't/won't, can't come here."

"Good old mother. Hey, who would have known that she had this inside her? She's never stuck up for us before, so I wonder why now."

"I don't know, and I don't really care, I'm just glad that she did, and at least we have one parent; now we just have to wait."

Chapter 6

It had been a long day, and the only thing I had to eat was gloopy porridge and a bacon butty and nothing else, and food was all I could think of. We had talked about the day's events, and I wasn't quite sure how this day would pan out, but I was hungry. Mrs F must have heard my tummy rumble as she started to cut the homemade bread, thick doorstop slices, my mouth was watering as she cut them. "Get the milk out of the fridge, and pour it into that pan," she ordered as she cut.

I quickly did as she said and poured the whole pint in a pan and put it on the stove. The bread had been cut and Mrs F put it on the brass forks which hung over the stove on some nails. "Here, you can be toasting them." She pushed them onto Fin as he sat in front of the fire. "Make yourself useful." She spoke. Both of us giggled slightly, then continued with our chores. Once the milk had boiled and bread was toasted, Mrs F smothered the bread in thick salty butter, placing it on dainty China plates before handing it to us, "You must be hungry," she scoffed a little, then continued making the hot chocolate. You would not believe that it was 2019, as Mrs F was like stepping back into time.

Mrs F's hot chocolate was the best, it wasn't Cadbury's; in fact, I didn't know what it was, I never saw the packet, but it was rich and chocolatey with a hint of spice. We both said thank you, then ate like we had never been fed. The day's events had been a little bizarre, taking twists and turns all over the place, I wasn't sure how it was going to end, but I trusted Immy and felt safe with Mrs F. For some reason, I have never seen father step one foot over this threshold, I've seen him at the door, but he has never come in. Mrs F was very old, I wonder why he feared her so much?

When we had finished eating, I washed up the cups and plates and put them on the shelves. There were no cupboards in the back pantry, just a sink and shelves, the shelves were heavily stocked, glass jars filled with jams, chutneys, marmalades, and whatever else was in them I didn't quite know, some look a tad old. Mrs F came in behind me and asked if I was OK and if I'd had enough to eat, her concern was welcoming, as she normally comes across as a bit rude and intolerant. "Yes, thank you, that was lovely, how long do you think they are going to be?"

"I don't know, child; it will take as long as long it takes and no longer," I heard what she said, but didn't really understand it, she often spoke in riddles, making things more complicated than they needed to be. "You know life has a funny way of turning out just as it is meant to, we see things for a reason, gifts are given to those who are worthy of them, don't ever forget that."

"I'm not sure I know what you mean" I replied faintly. For a short time, I thought I had seen a smile on her face, she never smiled, she only ever scowled; in fact, you seldom ever saw her face never mind a smile, her hunched shoulders meant her head looked at the floor, somehow removing the view of the world, but this never seemed to impede her. In fact, she knew things before others ever could, and she never went out the door?

Just as I gathered my thoughts and absorbed what Mrs F had said, the door burst open and in came Immy, her face reddened, her tousled locks hung like dead rats from her head. "What's happened?" I spurted. "Has he gone?" Fin just sat there quietly staring at the fire, looking like the stuffing had fallen out of him, my heart went out to him, we had done nothing wrong, today was an amazing day, why had it all gone pear shaped, I couldn't wrap my head around how quickly things had spiralled, and for what? Money?

Immy looked at us both, her energy shone around her, soft hues of pinks, all different types of pinks, making her face radiate. Her voice was low and slow, "Listen, you two, nothing you did today was wrong, and Fin you did amazing at the auction, but father's brother is a greedy man, always looking to make a fast buck wherever he can. When he recognised your name at the auction, he thought it was his duty to take, instead he just showed his true colours and scared a kid."

"But, Immy, he didn't threaten my life or anything, he just grabbed my arm and told me to sell direct to him in future." "Yes, Fin that's his way of saying, do it my way or else, he's a bully."

"Just like your father," Mrs F chirped in. "At least, people know what Jimmy is, who he is, he doesn't try to hide it, or be someone else." What is she talking about, is that another dig at father, what is it that father does that people don't know about, what is it that he hides? Immy shook her head at Mrs F, "Not now, Mrs F, it's not the time, they don't need to hear that." What was she talking about, why had she stopped Mrs F, from speaking the truth?

I'm more confused now than I was before, "So, what do we do? We can't stay here forever." I looked at Immy.

"No, Molly, I am taking you home, and all is going to be OK. Jimmy has gone, and mother and father are sat in the living room."

"Do they still want the money?" Fin asked.

"No, Fin, mother has talked father out of it, she told him that Hague kept the money and was saving it for you. Father won't dare go to a fellow farmer and ask for his son's money. Mother knows how to handle him."

"That's when she's awake, just wait till she goes to sleep, then she will be handled." Mrs F murmured under her breath, but loud enough for us to hear her. "Mrs F, that's enough. Come on, guys, we are going. Thank you, Mrs F, its greatly appreciated." Immy shot Mrs F a harsh glance and with that she grabbed our hands and lead us out the front door.

Mrs F stood at the door watching, her body somehow straightening as she raised her head to see us. I smiled and said thank you. We went into the small porch, kicked of our shoes adding them to an already sizable pile, then entered the living room. The smell of bodily odour and cigarettes was pungent, mixed in with some undistinguishable aftershave left by Jimmy. My body tensed, anticipating the roasting, but it didn't come, instead mother said, "Get your PJ's on, its bedtime." I looked at mother, her face was red and blotchy, it looks like she has been crying a lot, I felt bad for her. What had she gone through to save the day? But why had she had to go through anything, we hadn't done anything wrong, other than succeed.

Mother always built us up not to expect anything, saying you can't do that, you're not good enough to do that, who do you think you are, she would make us feel less than what we are. No expectations. But for me and Fin, it worked the other way; it made us defiant; it made us more determined to make something of our lives. For all I wished that I didn't live in the hell hole which I was born to, I also didn't take any notice of those around me, because normally, if they told you that you couldn't do something, it meant that you could, but they didn't want you to.

Oh, there was lots of manipulation in our childhood, reverse psychology they call it I think, and we fall right into the trap when mother does it, maybe it's because she knows we are defiant, and we are not going to follow her lead, maybe she needs us to be stronger than she is. I don't know the reason, but she's good at it. Fin went over to mother, gave her a hug and said night night, I had never done that, I normally just went to bed, but this night, I felt compelled to hug my mother, it felt a little strange, and I was afraid she would just push me away, but she didn't. Her warmth radiated into my energy field, it was kind and loving, I had never felt this before, probably because I had never hugged my mother before, her hand raised and touched the side of my face gently as she said night night, her green eyes glistened with tear drops, I replied, night night god bless, and gave her small kiss on her cheek.

As I turned to leave the room, father was lounged on the sofa, as if nothing had happened, but his face was as white as driven snow, his lips were pursed as his false teeth lay on the arm of the sofa, making his lips sunken, which made him look older. I looked at him and said nothing, his eyes stared right through me. What did Mrs F mean? I could see the swirling energy around father, dark browns, greys and black. I didn't know enough about the meaning of energy fields to read what this meant, but I could normally sense whether it was good or bad energy, and this was bad energy. The energy fields I saw were normally translucent, you could see through them; sometimes, energy glistens, but this energy field was opaque, there was no seeing through it, just darkness like a thunderous sky.

I went to the toilet, then up to bed. Nessa was already in bed; I cringed a little as I saw her. I quickly got into my night shorts, and hopped into bed, the house was quiet there was no Arty or Jay. I wonder where they are. "Night night, sleep well," Nessa said. I was taken aback, this day has been weird even for me, the whole dynamics of the family I thought I knew had changed; a mother I thought reviled me actually I think liked me, a brother I thought was tight with another brother was actually siding with mother, an evil uncle I had never heard of and a father who has secrets yet to be told, and to top it all of, no one had spoken about last night's events. I turned and said, "Night night," back to her, when I got a glimpse of her energy.

Nessa's energy field glowed radiant colours of the rainbow; every colour you could imagine emanated from her body I had never seen such beauty. "Why didn't you say anything about last night?" I murmured.

"There was nothing to say, I'm not sure what I saw, I was half asleep, and we all have the safe place that we go to. Molly, you will be OK, all will be OK, we will get out of this, and you will be safe."

"What do you mean?" There was no answer, as Nessa turned and fell to sleep.

I was a bit scared of going to sleep, what if it happened again, what did Nessa mean? So many questions were whizzing around my head, how to make sense of it all. Had it just been a dream, but what about today with Fin and Hague, what about the colours I'm seeing? So many questions and I didn't know where to begin. Soon, I was back, back in the meadow with the iridescent family of light; there appeared to be more light workers this time and their light shone brighter.

My body was soon left as I joined them, sensing their tension, my mind soon linked to the collective, which showcased their visions. Man turning against man, families turning against family, no trust, no love, no hope, as the darkness is consuming them one by one, taking their souls to the other side, to be dammed for eternity and beyond, no way out, no ascension, just a repeat of life on earth to do the bidding of the darkness and devour mankind as we know it.

Surely, we could do something, there had to be more light than darkness, but the universal balance was at risk, even though the light had mother and nature on its side, the darkness was consuming the human souls at a rapid rate. "Yes, but you're not thinking of this in a conscious way, think about what is being said, think about the way of the light, light works with nature, nature is free and unbound from man's restrictions, no matter how hard man tries, they won't break nature, its endless."

Collective: "Man is already breaking nature, drilling, mining, burying harmful products into its earth, man is not only destroying his own planet, but if it continues it will spread to the universe. We need man to awaken to what is occurring, it doesn't matter how many species or ancients we gather, man has been infected his DNA has been manipulated a long time ago. The Ori are now working with us to reverse what was done at the time of the Galactic war when the Prime Creator, Creator Gods nearly surrendered to the Egoiks".

Molly: "Whoa, now that's deep, man has enough just understanding of life; in fact, man is tired of trying to understand life, and its reasoning, man is ill-prepared and cannot fathom why he is even born. There is so much man does not know and will never know whilst living a human experience, but this isn't what man was meant to be."

"Man cannot keep being born into these lifetimes trying to remember why they went there in the first place, they are looking for a way out, this is why the darkness is so appealing, I know because I felt it beckoning to me too."

"Maybe the light needs to lead, instead of pushing from an unknown place which is unreachable by man." I could hear their chatter and could feel their excitement welling up like excited young children pulling at their mothers' arm. Their vibration was raised and along with it, the vibration of the forest as it hummed with life, everywhere I looked, the light radiated to the sky and beyond, causing a rainbow effect.

Collective: "It was agreed many eons ago that the family of light were not able to show themselves to man, they were only able to guide or sometimes heal. There are many differing species which assist earth and man, but the Egoiks have broken their agreement, they tire at man's defiance, and want to control man like they control their own race with one mind. The Egoiks are not happy that man has freedom of choice, but this is a freedom planet, and not one race can change that. However, if the Egoiks turn man into pure ego, then the soul will be cast into purgatory, never able to return home to their place of origin."

My mind wandered as I immersed in the eternal love of the family of light; I wished I could stay here, even though I now knew my path, and knew my destiny, I had nothing else to work for, but I still had to continue my life on earth, before I could ascend, I still had to make it through, without breaking.

Surely, this time it would be easier, I know where I am from and why I am here, I will encourage man to stay on light's path, be at peace with nature, and embrace what the universe provides, but the Collective also needs to be at one with man and nature, working in harmony to avoid universal crisis.

The light needs to shine and lead the way, the light needs to show itself to the world instead of hiding in the shadows of the darkness, the light has allowed the darkness to consume.

Collective: "Hey, hold on, I can hear your thoughts, the light never shows itself to man, life is a choice of a light worker."

Molly: "Yeh yeh, I hear you, and then the soul is born and spends the rest of its life trying to remember why it was born in the first place. Whose idea was this anyway? You would think I would know that answer, seem as I as old as time, some things I remember and some things are still coming to me; remembering 360 lifetimes on earth is pretty daunting, but also exhilarating. But life is hard enough to live, without having to fulfil a life's task which you have no knowledge of, would it not be simpler if the process was a little easier?"

Collective: "It would be easier, and simpler, but life isn't about simplicity, it's about fulfilling your life's potential, growing and developing."

Molly: "Yes, I get that, but a solution needs to be found; man cannot continue to be bound by the task of life, or he will surely turn to the darkness." I could sense the trepidation in what I was saying, but these souls had not been down to earth in a long time and the earth has changed, man has changed. Even though the balance of the universe is at risk, the energy of the world has changed, where love tries to prevail, the darkness absorbs, they are fighting a losing battle and need help. "All I ask is that the process is made a little easier, not too easy, just a way for man to reconnect to the source, in the hope that he can find his way home sooner, he can see the light, which would drown out the darkness."

A calmness washed over me, and a conscious decision was made, man would be led to the light through nature, being at one with nature. "So, am I right in thinking that if we get man to reconnect to nature, that they would be shown the light, therefore remember the way of the light and why they went to earth in the first place?"

Collective: "No, we can only guide man to learn how to see the light through nature, and reconnect to the light source of the universe, but there is no way, we can assist man to fulfil his life's task, that will be up to him. You forget that each light worker reborn does so with the assistance of six other light workers; these light workers reside here, whilst guiding their soul on the path of enlightenment. However, they cannot intervene in man's path, and they cannot disclose themselves, as that will break the code which we agreed to in the great surrender."

Molly: "Well, obviously that isn't working, I have never sensed another soul beside me, other than Red Clogs in the attic, and I'm certain that's just a fable my brothers made up to scare me." Emotions ran torrent in me, whilst I felt the calmness, my frustration to find the answer for man was growing; they say they can guide but cannot show man, they showed me.

Collective: "You forget how we communicate here, we know what you are thinking, as you are thinking, we can hear the words like you are communicating."

Ugh, I snapped out of my thoughts. "Oh, I forget you are in my head, that's a bit invasive isn't it, why can't I hear you all the time, why aren't your minds as busy as mine?"

Collective: "Our communication works in a different way; we will tell you about that another day. Right now, we need to agree to the mission, as we cannot move forward without your consent like we cannot enter a home without being invited, etc etc."

Molly: "Yes, you are right, but you must realise I am yet to learn of the old way, I still cannot remember my past lives, and I don't have the wisdom of the ages, I am still only 14 years old! But I do know one thing, it will take more than guiding man to nature and showing him through mother earth." Wow, where did that come from, did I just call earth mother? Well, obviously, that's what it is called on earth, but here too, is mother 'actually' the creator?

Collective: "Yes, she is definitely one of them, mother is one of the creators of life, she is also the caretaker of life, not unlike a mother who cares and loves her children, doing anything to protect them."

Well, I would have found that hard to believe yesterday, as my mother was the punisher, the persecutor, but what I've seen in the last 24 hours makes me think differently, maybe mothers are the caregivers, maybe they just forget their role too?

This is getting too complex for words, my 14-year-old self is muddled, yet my wiser older being is calm; I feel both as they battle for control, wondering which one will reside.

Collective: "Maybe there is a way, one where man can connect to mother quicker." I listened with intent, awaiting the answer of the collective, but there was silence.

"Which way is this?" I was asking.

Still silence as the Collective seemed to be communicating without my knowledge. I wonder how they are doing this; how can they exclude me from the conversation. Then without realising, I could see their thoughts, visualising the past, present and the future; they were communicating in picture, I hadn't allowed myself to see, but I was still using an element of mind, instead of being pure presence, thus when my mind had calmed, I could see all. It was tragic what had become of man, sad even, how they had destroyed each other's morality of living, and persecuted the difference.

The Collective spoke, "We have tried showing man the way; we have sent souls to earth with the full knowledge of their mission, with full knowledge of where they came from and what the outcome was, you were once part of this process and even in that life, it was not achieved. Man didn't take too kindly to their words, and it ended in blood being shed." I could see the images of men and women being tortured, but to what avail? Man, simply couldn't handle the truth, the true light which is within them is dimmed by control of those who seek control and power; these men are filled with fear and rage, the only way they can live is to control others. "But what about the way man can connect with mother quicker?" Still no answer, and the darkness came, I awoke filled with questions, yet this was not to be as the question was left hanging.

Chapter 7

Well, at least I awoke of my own accord, no shaking, no slapping, no screaming. I looked around and all was quiet, sisters slumbered in the beds beside me. What was this day to bring? Thoughts of the past 24 hours filled me with horror; I looked over to see Immy's bed, empty, she must be up already. Immy starts work at 6 am; she works in an old factory which is a massive textile factory owned by the Hemmington family. The factory is filled which huge looms, imposing and deafening to the naked ear. I had been into the factory only once; I was given earmuffs to cover my ears, as I stood among the great looms. I can remember feeling very small, rows and rows of giant pieces of machinery, the looms going back and forth, the workers guiding them into place so as they made the perfect cloth. This was no ordinary weaving mill, it was one of the last mills in the country, which had been brought into the twenty-first century, run by computers and machines, the millers only there to guide.

Immy was cloth designer, she seemed to enjoy her time at work; I never once heard her moan about the hours or pay; in fact, I never heard her moan about anything, she seemed to sail through life, knowing what she wanted, not tainted by the expectations of others. Her boyfriend was a biker, he was funny and accepting, yet mother and father didn't appear to like him, like he wasn't good enough or something, but Immy was happy when she was with him, and her love for him shone from within. Her eyes would glisten as she gazed at him, her love would overflow, why couldn't mother and father see this, maybe it's because they had never felt that love?

Mother was the seventh child of 11, raised in a wealthy farming family, attending a private school, what was expected of her, was not what she gave her parents. Mother was a beautiful young lady, winning carnival queen in the village where she was raised. When she was crowned, she was given a stunning necklace with clusters of clear diamonds, with a bright blue sapphire in the centre. The necklace was always spoken about, but I had never seen it. Mother could have married any man in the village, her stunning red hair and green eyes, her chiselled cheeks and strong jaw line, made her a natural beauty, her sisters always said she was the most beautiful, but somehow, I never saw that person, time had changed her, or maybe father had changed her.

When they met, father was 21, he was five years older, which was nothing in those days, older men would often marry younger ladies. My father was the youngest child in his family, and he was spoilt. Apparently, he had been a sickly child, and grew up jaundice, he was yellow, mmm maybe there was a reason for this, maybe that's his true colour, the colour of a coward. Rant over, let's get back to it, father rarely went out, he had few friends and chose to stay at his father's side most of the time. Grandfather was a fruitier, delivering fruit and vegetables to markets, like his father who delivered fruit with a pony and trap, father says the horses were high steppers, but in the pictures, they just looked like regular ponies.

Father always made his family out to be better than mothers, as if it was a competition, one which mother would never win. His father's heritage came from the gypsies of Irish decent. I have heard him talk of his father many times, but he doesn't talk about his mother very often, like she never existed. The only story I have heard is that she was a dancer in a local town, which grandfather tamed. When he recites the story, it's as if he is proud of his father's achievements, taming a lady. Maybe that's why father has no respect for ladies, he chooses to own or control women them rather than love them, using them like pawns in a game of life.

Mother's parents apparently didn't agree with their matching and did all they could to keep mother away from father, but it didn't work. Mother was defiant, steadfast in her choosing, then she disgraced the family by getting pregnant out of wedlock. Mother left the large family estate, swapping it for a two-bed terraced in a neighbouring town, having her first born when she was 18, then went on to have another six children in a spate of 10 years. Mother's father died before I was born, as had my father's parents, so I never got to meet them. I recollect some pictures of them though. Father's father was a tall slender man, not like father who is small and feeble; he stood tall wearing a white grocer's overcoat, and an old trilby hat, his mother was tall too, yet she was frailer, and had a sadness about her. I wonder what they would think of father today.

When my parents are arguing, I can hear the spite in my mother's voice, filled with regret of what could have been, how her life could have so much better had she have not met father. He would spit back at her that her family was nothing, but a bunch of crooks and liars, maybe he is talking about his own family, because mother's brothers and sisters are lovely; they have pride and respect, they don't hide in the shadows or try to control their partners. I have parents who argue a lot, their words are mean and unloving; mothers' words can cut like a knife, her tongue is like a serpent's bite, I suppose this is her only tool.

Father chooses to control mother with fear of loss, saying she would have nothing without him, she would have no money, no home. He was right, but sometimes to have nothing is to have more, nothing would be better than living a life of lies. Mother always backed down, always forgave his infidelities or his unkind words; she was always the little woman who raised her family to be strong and resilient, and to stand in the face of adversity. Maybe that's why she is so harsh, maybe that's why she chooses to reprimand so much, it's her way of teaching her children how to cope, how to stand up for what they believe in and never back down.

Immy was doing just that, she was standing up for what she believed in, and her belief was Tee short for Teelan. My mind was cast back to a few weeks ago when we visited Aunty Ju to try on the dresses for Immy's wedding; it was a wonderful day, one which I will cherish, a day which had given me peace. Even though mother didn't agree with Immy's choice of husband, she still supported her, and wanted the best for her; that's probably why her sister Ju made the dress, I still remember the day.

Mothers' youngest sister Ju was a seamstress for royalty and worked in the capital; she was so elegant, and wore the most amazing clothes, I was in awe of her appearance, and thought one day, I would be like her. Ju had bleach blonde hair, not unlike my own which was natural; she wore little, or no makeup and her outfits were always different which made her stand out against the rest, the best thing about Aunty Ju was her footwear; no matter what she wore on her body, she always wore boots on her feet, be it summer or winter.

The boots were outlandish, with diamantes and coloured stones, different style stitching or uses of material, they were sometimes gaudy, but never cheap, I absolutely loved them. Aunty Ju was my favourite aunty, one I aspired to be like. Mothers' other family members are lovely too, but Aunty Ju sets a president. I have only been to her apartment once; she lives beside the water, as her husband races motorboats and docks at the marina outside their apartment. They live a lavish lifestyle, their apartment is minimalistic with little furniture, leaving large open spaces, everything is clean and tidy and there is a place for everything.

Aunty Ju had greeted us at the reception to the building; she hugged us all, but extended the hug for her sister, whom she held for just a bit longer, I remember watching her as she held her sister in her loving grasp. We went up to the apartment in the elevator which was hung on an external wall with glass overlooking the estuary, everything about this venue screamed wealth. I just loved it, and soaked up every minute, the smile never left my face. Aunty Ju's sewing room is large, with a chaise lounge in one corner and a changing area in the other, the changing area is a screen with exotic designs printed all over it, the most opulent colours, as the metallic thread shines and glistens from the sun peering through the big glass window. The large window lets the natural day light in allowing her to see material in its natural beauty, her choices of cloth were rich and expensive, her workmanship exhibited all over the apartment, documented through canvas and tapestry.

Aunty Ju's work resonated through our bridesmaids' dresses which were different to say the least; they were white with metallic blue spots, tiny metallic spots which made your eyes go fuzzy if you looked at them too long, they hung just past the knee on the calf; I felt they were a little old fashioned, but Aunty Ju assured Immy that they were the up-and-coming fashion led from Milan and Paris. I giggled as she said this, thinking I was going to be a catwalk model. Immy placed the dress over my head, making certain my grubby hands didn't touch it, or mark it, as if I hadn't cleaned my hands, which I 'definitely' had, but just to be on the safe side.

It was refreshing to visit Aunty Ju, no farm, no mess, no arguments, it was just me, Immy, mother and Nessa. This was the first time I had ever been out with mother and two sisters and the first time I had ever been to the capital. The happiness and joy had filled me up, as I was finally free from the restrictions of home, no rules, no arguing, just five members of the same family having a lovely day out. The capital captivated my heart, I could feel its pulse beating, the energy it omitted was extreme, it wasn't only the capital, it was the origin of our fine country.

I remembered feeling somewhat proud to be in this astonishing place, surrounded by artists and scholars alike. The architecture leant to each creator; the personality portrayed within it. I could see myself living here, where the power lay, and the decisions of the country were made. Monumental buildings, extravagant clothes, wealth was dripping from every lamppost, building and being.

Aunty Ju had lived here from being married at 18; she attended rich galas with powerful people, her dresses were desired by the elite, her husband's career was followed by those who sought to support him, in the hope that money was to be made.

I was in awe and wondered if one day, I could aspire into this world, maybe I could leave my humble life behind and follow in the footsteps of my aunty.

Maybe this is what mother once desired, or maybe she was destined to be right where she is. The day soon passed; Immy drove us home in Erbies car which she had borrowed, all happy and content in the knowledge that we had completed Immy's wedding task. I remember that day like it was yesterday, it fed my soul, helping me to believe in the impossible, after all, if Aunty Ju had done it, so could I.

As I emptied my porridge into the bowl, my thoughts were interrupted as a door banged. I looked around but saw no one, maybe it was just the wind. I got back to the task at hand, getting the syrup out of the cupboard. The bottom of the tin had stuck to the shelf, making it difficult to pull out, then I felt the presence as father stood there behind me. The energy was dark, it hadn't changed in presence, yet it felt more dangerous. I turned, observed him and said, "Good morning."

His gaze hit me like a ton of bricks, the darkness radiated through his eyes. Normally, his eyes were bright blue, like crystals glistening in the sunlight, today there was no light, not one iota. What had happened? In came mother and the energy darkened even more; it felt like father had grown another foot, as his anger flowed through him. His dark eyes stabbed at mother; no words were spoken. The air was thick, I felt like I couldn't breathe as if the air was withdrawing from the room, making an airtight capsule, but that was impossible; the window was open, the air should flow through here like it always had, yet all the air had withdrawn, folded back like an endangered animal, leaving so as it could save itself. Its lack of presence didn't seem to affect mother or father; their energy was like death anyway.

I contemplated speaking to break the awkward silence but decided to conserve energy until my breath had returned. I ditched the syrup and took my bowl to the table. Still catching my breath, watching mother and father like a hawk, wondering where this was going to end. So much for the beautiful recollection of the day in the capital, I wished I could be transported back there. Mother was so peaceful that day, not like today, her energy was sad and broken, she was broken.

Mother stood at the kitchen sink, her bathrobe draping over her sunken body. What had happened last night, would I ever know how mother got father to back down. Looking down at my porridge, I noticed blood on mother's foot. Had she cut herself? I scanned the bottom of her legs, her left leg was black and blue, what had she done? I knew better than to ask, my stomach knotted, what had she endured to protect me and Fin?

Hurriedly, I finished my porridge; I needed to get out of this room, the energy was toxic, draining my soul. There was nothing I could do about mother, she wouldn't tell me what had happened, so I might as well just leave it. Standing up to place my bowl in the sink, mother's subtle energy touched me; her gaze held mine just for a second, she appeared to reassure me, her eyes telling me that it was going to be OK.

Leaving the contaminated kitchen sent a wave of relief over my body, phew thank God, that's over, but what would the day bring? It was a beautiful morning, the sun was rising from its slumber, just peeking out from its covers of darkness, shedding light on a new day. The grass was dewy, its crystals sparkling with the light of the sun's new rays; there was a cool breeze rustling through the trees, making leaves fall softly to the ground. Autumn was coming, the end of the summer was upon us and soon, we would be heading into winter.

I didn't much like the winter months; the days were too short, but I always felt that winter was like a foundation for spring. Spring was beautiful here on the farm, dressing the garden with lush grass rich foliage, and array of colours from the new spring plants which awaken from their hibernation. Spring always gave me a sense of hope; hope that one day, things would be different; hope that one day, I would leave this forsaken house and maybe have a garden of my own.

Caught up in my own thoughts of seasons and weather, I didn't notice Fin walking towards me, his presence always seemed to catch me of guard. "Morning!" he bellowed, making me jump out of my skin. I looked up and saw his cheeky grin. "Oh, good morning, what are you up to today?" My gut twisted with the thoughts of yesterday's events; I hoped today was going to be a bit calmer. "Nothing much, we have some cabins to muck out and the muck trailer is coming at 10, so I need to muck out before it comes."

Cringing at the thought of loading a muck trailer, or emptying chicken poop from cabins, "I think I will give that a miss."

"I thought you would say that you don't like getting your hands dirty, do you?" Scowling at his comment I smirked a little, as it was true; not that I didn't like to get my hands dirty, but I really didn't like cow or chicken muck, its pungent smell of muck and ammonia would stay with me for days. "I have two lawns to mow before the wet weather sets in. I need to mow for Bell and Mrs F, and it looks like it's going to be a dry day, so better get them done before school next week."

Fin didn't like school, any chance to have the day off, he would take it. I wondered if he would ever learn to read or write, but I'm sure that no matter what he does in life, he will do OK. That's if father doesn't get in the way; father was always expecting too much of Fin, he is only 14, nearly 15 years old, and runs a farm; he would be very successful if he had his own farm, maybe one day he would.

"How did you sleep, any weirder dreams?"

"Err well, yes, but no talking and definitely no glowing. You know, they communicate via the mind, they don't have a mouth."

Fin looked at me in that dumb way. "Well, I never thought a beam of light would have a mouth. What did they tell you this time? That you were God or something."

"No! I'm not talking about this with you, you don't believe in that stuff."

"No, but I'm trying, Molly, it's difficult to believe that we are led by these light people you talk about, and if we don't find the light, we are all doomed."

Hearing the words spoken like that did make it seem a little farfetched. "I know what you mean, I would never have believed it myself, but there has to be more to this world, it can't just be birth, life and then death, what comes after, why are we here, and why the bloody hell did we choose to be born into this family?"

"Well, Molly, if you ask me, life is rubbish; you live, you die, and then nothing. What else could there possibly be? You go to heaven and sit on a cloud all day, or you go the depths of hell, and relive your worst nightmare. I just don't know what to believe; at church they talk about God, and what you have to do to go to heaven, or if you sin, you go to hell, there is no mention of light people."

"Yeh, I know, it's hard to digest, but maybe the church doesn't want people to know the truth, or maybe 'they' don't know the truth, or don't choose to believe the truth, they just want to spout their version of the truth, a truth which is more believable. The light workers work on behalf of the creator; they are the ones who guide us, or so they say."

"Well, they are doing a bang-up job, most people I know are just getting by some are so screwed up that they take drugs or drink to forget. Who is guiding them?"

My thoughts drifted back to the conversation with the light workers, how we discussed the possibility of showing their light, and guiding the way in a more meaningful manner, where people know they exist. Maybe then people will have hope in the future, maybe they will remember why they are here, maybe they will not feel like failures? Oh, so many maybes so many what ifs, so many questions.

"Hoy, day dreamer, pass me that fork. Where did you go?"

"Nowhere, I was just thinking. What if things were different, what if people actually knew why they were born, maybe there would be less pain." Smiling. I passed him the fork, and he started to rake up the chicken dung. Fin kept his chickens very clean, there wasn't much poop, so I began to help shovelling it into the barrow; I would get out the way when he did the calve pens. The calve bedding was a lot heavier than the chicken poop, calves were bed on straw, their beds weren't mucked out daily like the chickens, a calve bed was deep, as they were only mucked out when the calves had been sold or gone to slaughter. Father used to complain about Fin using too much straw, as he used it to top the calve beds up every other day, when he would spread a fresh layer of straw, they may not have been mucked out, but Fin always made certain they were comfortable and not lying in their own dung.

Fin broke the silence, "Well, yesterday was a peculiar day."

"You can say that again, I didn't know that father had another brother. That Jimmy is something isn't he?"

"Mmmm but I should have known it would have something to do with father, he just can't abide anyone else doing better than him, I wouldn't mind he's not even a farmer, he doesn't know what a fork is, or how to use one."

Father delivered bread for a living, he was out early in the morning to deliver to the shops around the city; then I don't know what he did, because he never came home until nightfall, sometimes, 8 pm sometimes, 10 pm. I never knew that there was so much bread to deliver, he was rarely home, even at weekends, he wasn't present, that is until lately.

Chapter 8

As we finished mucking out the chicken shed, Fin had a look of concern. "Why do you think father was home yesterday; it can't be because of the money I made at the market."

"I don't know why he was home; it wasn't normal, he doesn't normally come home before dark. Why, what are you thinking?"

"I'm thinking that I hope this isn't the new norm, it's hard enough having him bust my ear at night or the odd weekend I see him, without seeing him every day, he makes my blood boil."

I could see that Fin was becoming anxious, as he struggled talking when he was getting wound up or upset. Day to day, you couldn't notice his slight stutter, but when father was in the mix, Fin found it difficult to string two words together. Father used to gaud him, stuttering back in a childish manner, it's hard to imagine that he fathered seven children, and that despite everything, we have turned out OK, well-mannered and polite, well at least I think so.

My heart went out to Fin, I could see his worry, and felt his pain. "Don't worry, all will be OK." Fin managed a smile in reply.

"What happened last night, did you hear anything, was mother OK?" I finally asked, I had wanted to ask all morning, but the timing was never quite right.

"What do you mean?" Fin asked sheepishly, "What did you hear?"

"It's quite obvious that I heard nothing if I am asking you what happened. After Immy brought us home, I went to bed, and it was lights out." I found myself questioning my words, is that all that happened? What about Nessa, and how she was with me, how kind she had been, that was weird, but I didn't bother mentioning it, as Fin seemed to have enough on his mind.

Fin finally replied, after quiet contemplation, he spurt out a secret I'm sure he wasn't meant to disclose to me. Fin was bitter, hurt and angry, he lashed out at his father, spilling the sordid secret of father's bedroom antics. "We all know what happens to mother when she doesn't abide by father's words." "What?" I asked eagerly. What happens, they argue, they fight, my mind was running rampant about all the possibilities which father could do to mother, then Fin replied. "He beats her, you know; sometimes, I hear her sobbing till early morning. I don't know how he stops her from screaming but he does, she has muffled screams, he thinks we can't hear it, but we are right next door, and its heart breaking." Fin's eyes are filled with tears at the recollection of his mother's pain. "Honestly, Molly. I don't know how she puts up with it, I just want to stop him, I hate him for what he does."

My stomach knotted as I recollect the conversation with Mrs F and how she had spoken about father, she didn't like him much; well actually, she didn't like him at all, even that comment is an understatement. Mrs F couldn't stand the man, and I never knew why, well now I do, this makes more sense, the reason she was so protective of mother.

"Are you sure father beats mother? I've never seen any bruising, on her face or anywhere."

"No, you won't see a bruise on the face; he doesn't seem to mark anywhere which is visible to others, why do think she rarely wears shorts, or dresses, her legs are black and blue, and you don't want to see her body."

Still pondering Fin's wild remarks, I got to thinking of all the times I had noticed a change in her, the mood swings when father was home, the fear, or apprehension of his return to home, and now he is home again, on a weekday, this is unheard of. So, how must she be feeling, why doesn't she just leave him? They only argue when he is home, then the day after, they don't speak, so I guess that's after the beating, what a way to live, that's no life, no wonder she is so God damn sad.

"This morning, I saw blood on mothers' foot, I didn't ask her what it was, as father was there, now that I come to think of it, she looked in pain."

"Yep, I don't know what they were doing last night, there were a lot of muffled sounds, you know I'm sure he covers her mouth, or puts a pillow over her face. It's awful to hear, some nights I just lay there holding the knife under my pillow, one day, I swear, I will end it."

"Oh, my goodness, Fin, is it that bad, why didn't you ever tell me?"

"You are too young, and you don't need that shit, Fin turned saying, I have no choice, I sleep in the room next door." My head was still trying to grasp his words, rage consumed me. I felt so bloody angry and frustrated; I might be 14, but I'm the oldest soul in this house, why hadn't I seen what was happening?

My abilities are still tuning to the light where I originated from, I can see more energy fields, my senses are heightened, yet I could not see what was in front of me, happening in my own home. If I have had so many life experiences on earth, you would think I would recognise when a mother is covering up a beating.

I felt enraged by what I had learnt, I have been here 359 times, on this earth. Now, I chose to come back again for the 360th time. Why the bloody hell would anyone in the right mind do that? I could have ascended, I could have left the souls to live their lives, then one day ascend, knowing that they would achieve it in the end as I had done.

But life on earth was getting harder, the world was developing at a rapid rate, increasing the pressure placed upon the souls. What was this going to achieve? Men, women, and children were beginning to show weakness, they were conforming to the spouted words of world leaders, believing they weren't good enough, they were sinners, destined for hell. Their hearts were dying, along with their souls, as the darkness consumed them. What was this bloody life about? The souls on earth had chosen to be born into a hell hole, why?

My God, what are you doing? Whoever the bloody creator is, you need a lesson in fathering, no father would put their child through so much pain, and no child should have to prove their worthiness to a father, so what the hell is going on? I was consumed by questions, as I scooped more poop the questions kept coming, and anger raged within.

Creator: "So, what would you have me do? Every time, I have tried to show the way to the people of the earth, they have killed every messenger; they have twisted every word, they have misconstrued every message sent to them. So, tell me what would you have me do? How do I mend the souls, how do I prevent them from turning to the darkness? The balance of the universe is at great risk, too many souls are taking their own lives, or the lives of others in so many ways, man is turning against man, or worse against himself, you are there as the final message."

What! I scuttle round, searching for whoever was speaking, there was no one there, now that's it, I'm losing my bloody mind. Fin looked at me.

"What's the matter, you're jumping around like you've just been bitten on the butt."

"Did you just hear that, there was a man talking."

"Molly, you're losing the plot, you need more sleep or something."

"No no no no, I'm telling you there was a man talking, I heard him as clear as day."

"It's one of your light friends, you know the ones you visit in your sleep," with a chuckle Fin goes to the calve pens. Watching him leave, he threw both arms up in the air, and shouted, "Whatever."

Maybe he was right, calming my mind, I tried to listen for their communication, but nothing.

Creator: "Are you ready, Molly? This is your final life on earth, this is your choice."

I let the panic subside and stopped flapping around like a manic bird to listen. I knew what he was saying, and I knew who it was, father, the creator, the originator, the big boss, source. Was this the final reckoning?

Molly: "Why are you here? The light workers had given me the message loud and clear, and now you."

Source: "I get your frustration, Molly, you have lived many lives, seeing and experiencing man in all his glory, you have never given up on the possibility of man, always believing that man can live in peace and harmony, you constantly disobey the Collective to ascend and continue to live on earth, despite the fact that you have already fulfilled your life's task, whilst running the risk of soul burn out."

Molly: "Yes, I know, that's because I believe in man. I think man has had a raw deal from the start of time. How was man meant to succeed when his father was deemed to be a great punisher, when his father judged so harshly banishing his two new-borns from a beautiful garden because they ate an apple? Then man tearing each other apart to find the one true God, thinking that the creator can, save them, if they had a clear message then they could survive, they can live in peace. If they knew the truth."

Source: "1. Adam nor Eve were banished from the garden; they returned to the light, having lived many lives since, then ascending to the source, and sit with the Ancients, you know this, Molly, you know the truth, you know the answers, but can you give the message clearly enough, can you tell man the truth?"

2. "Man created his own perception of the creator of the universe, this was man's word, they chose to turn the creator into the almighty to create fear, controlling man's mind to keep man in check. This was not our doing; this was not our intention. Ever since the sending of the first messenger, the Egoiks have thwarted our ploy to awaken man to his origin. They are always quick to disarm the truth and manipulate it

to control man, but earth is meant to be a FREE WILL planet. Man has been manipulated since the great surrender, and sadly, we have not retaliated in fear of our own planet's eradication, but now things are different; the planets have aligned, advancements have been made. We are finally able to protect ourselves and earth. We are now ready and able to fight if we must, and we will return man to his form of origin. So, are you going to finally save man? First you need save yourself, you have to remember who you were when you were born before the great surrender."

Molly: "I don't know how to do that, the light workers are no help, they tell me what needs to be done, but I am only 14 years old on earth; what can I possibly do to help man? I can't even help my own mother."

Source: "Remember, you are what you believe you are, you do what you believe you do, you are the creators of your own reality."

Molly: "Really! Oh, now, that's just great. I am my own creator. Are you having a laugh? If I was my own creator, I would be happy, I would have loving parents, I would want for nothing, and not have to worry about being punched daily. I would have money and enough to eat, so you are telling me a 14-year-old girl that I am my own creator!"

I could feel the emotions well up, overflowing in venomous spite, all the pain pouring out of my voice, the anger and resentment at the words being spoken to me. I felt enraged, how the hell could I be my own creator, would I really create this sh*t? Jesus, I didn't even want to be here, never mind remembering past lifetimes.

With venom and bitterness, I continued to spit out the hurt I felt at his guidance. "First, you tell me that I need to connect to the source to remember my lifetimes, to remember the truth about the creation of the universe. The creation of man and why I crave to help man so much, oh and while we are talking, you say I am my own creator, which, makes it all the worse. I cannot remember any of what you say and who the hell is the Collective?" Feeling the anger, I just wanted to lash out, I wanted to scream, I wanted to yell, I wanted to punch something. The unjustness of what I had been told, the resentment grew and so did my anger. Now, I knew why my mother projected her feelings so much, she was unable to unleash them onto the persecutor, so she unleashed them onto me instead, a defenceless child, the pain within was unbearable, what was it all about?

Source: "Molly, seek and you will find"

Infuriated by this line, I could feel the frustration rising, face reddening, then no more. *Seek and you will find*, I've heard that saying many times before, when things are lost, mother would always say it, "Seek and you will find," and true enough, it would be found, but does the same apply to life?

Lost in my own thoughts, I left Fin and started walking. I headed down the yard towards the back fence, it was always the quickest way to get to the open fields, leaving the confines of home far behind. The fence was made up of all sorts, netting, old wood, pallets, and metal sheets, anything but the normal fence materials, so it was easy to find the gap and slip between. This led onto a narrow path which was shaded by overhanging leaves from the old oaks and beech blocking out the direct sun but leaving enough rays to illuminate the way.

The peaceful tranquillity of the stream surrendered itself to my presence, welcoming me with a dance and melodic tune. Feeling its welcoming embrace, I smiled, as if to say thank you, watching its rhythmical radiance as it elegantly rolled by, jumping from one stepping stone to another to avoid interruption of its rhythm, I crossed to the other side. The path widened, with a grass verge sloping down to the water's edge. I walked slowly by its side, enjoying the ambiance of the location. Leaving the path, I strolled up a grass incline, covered by trees which seemed to whisper silently to me.

Come forward, I could hear their words, come. Cautiously, I continued through the wooded incline, until it opened to a wide expanse of stunning meadow. I have played here many times, rolling from the top of the incline down the hill, feeling the freshness of the ground before me, smelling its sweet aroma of freshly cut grass lying on the field waiting to be collected by the farmer.

I felt at home here, the caution subsided, leaving a peaceful sensation deep within. The trees kept calling, 'come forward.' I stood, opened my arms wide to feel the autumnal breeze flow through my body, filling me up with energy and light, mother's caress was warm and gentle, the loving embrace of all she has to give. Nature with nature, one animal to another, I sat appreciating all that mother nature provided us with now and in the past, how she has taken care of me, hidden me when I've needed to get away, been my solace in a crazy world, mother nature is the constant, forever changing, but always there.

Breathing in all her brilliance, reconnecting to the place of origin, I left my 14-year-self, ascending to the light where I had originated. I could see my body sitting there in wonder, her face like an angel, her hair as white as snow, why had I chosen her to be my vessel, what would she grow into?

Like a laser across a night's sky, I shot of, launched into a past dimension, one of glitz and glamour, cast into a glamorous party. Gargoyles perched on the two towers at the front of the building, the large glass doors were framed with gold, allowing the light to shine through, bouncing of the gold lighting the street in front. Where was this place? Why had I come here? Blending in with the light, I entered the building.

The host was welcoming guests to the party, this was a formal gathering; the men wore black suites and dicky bows, whilst the ladies donned long evening dresses, laden with jewels and diamonds, this was a fanciful event, but why was I here?

Light Guide: "You're here to see what your past lives look like."

"Who are you?"

Light Guide: "I am your guide, when you chose to be born, there were six other light workers with you, it is our job to keep you on the right track for you to achieve the life's goal."

Molly: "Yes, but I didn't make that goal. did I? Because I went too soon."

Light Guide: "That may be the case, but you had spoken about saving man from man for many generations, and that has always been your goal before of which you have achieved in many lifetimes, yet you always choose to return, as man always finds a way of disrupting the process. In previous lives, your goal has always been to guide man and save him from himself, supporting man to be humble and wise, to help others, spreading the light and the joy."

"Your light shines brighter than them all, you have the power and the ability to guide man into the light, averting the temptation of the darkness, you're not going to give up now."

Molly: "How long have you been my light guide?"

Light Guide: "I joined you in your last lifetime, that is why I am here; there are many souls who guide, you have been a soul mate to many souls too, and you have helped them to ascend, that is the job of the soul mate or light guide, helping another to fulfil their destiny and ascend. But your case is different, as you have already got the magic ticket to ascension, yet you choose to help man, but this is your last lifetime. The Collective have spoken and request your presence, you knew this before you returned, you accepted the wishes of the Collective and creator Gods and knew this was your last lifetime."

Molly: "Can I ask? What's the point of remembering the past when I don't even remember how the hierarchy of our world works, and what is it going to change, how can remembering the past help save the future?"

At that point, our light joined, helping me see and feel his words, remembering everything about where we came from, our missions, our collective family and father, so the narrative goes. "In laymen's terms, we have Havenmoor, where the souls rest whilst making their decision to birth, then we have the source (man's heaven which is where you ascend to, your place of origin). We have a leaders, known as the creator gods and Prime is the leader we call Father, and Father is led by a board called the Collective, then we have the Federation of Light. The federation is made up of many different species, some look like man, others have alternative features, greys, birds, fish, they represent the building blocks of the earth.

They are the wisest and most enlightened beings and known as the masters. Their energy is the all-powerful, as they are all conscious beings; leading through consciousness, they have the ability to speak as one, as they and we are all interconnected. They also lead the light workers (known to you as souls), the souls help keep the balance of good and bad in the universe."

Light Guide: "That's a brief rundown of the hierarchy of the light; to maintain the light we need the balance of good and bad. You can choose to have a bad life experience, you can choose to do bad things in your life's journey, but you always come back to the light, and if you do, then you get to go home and that's your life's journey fulfilled."

Light Guide: "It's ironic, isn't it, that we would choose to experience bad thigs in our lives, but we do, as those experiences help you to develop and grow, evolving into the person, being, you always wanted to be. This choice isn't an easy choice for a light worker, as they do it at great risk, to both themselves and the source, as the darkness could consume them, and they would be lost forever, never able to return to the light."

Light Guide: "The importance is choice; they had to have a choice, be it good or bad, and no matter what that choice was, they could return to the light, if they had achieved their life's goal. I know what you're thinking, well that isn't right, how can you possibly return to the light, even if you have been bad? What if you have killed someone? The top and bottom of it is that there is a reason for everything, and in choosing a bad life, then returning to the light helps you gain more brownie points with the Collective, as it shows strength and determination to return to the light, instead of surrendering to the darkness. Helping to develop your skills to become a master, knowing that light is always the source and from the source."

Reflecting upon what my light guide was saying, I felt the presence of the light within me, I returned to the party, in remembrance of my past life.

Chapter 9

Back at the party, the hostess turned to greet a guest. My goodness, she was beautiful, graceful, and loving, her success hung to her like her dress. The understated power, she wore a stunning gown, made of fine gold and silver thread, carrying it like a princess. The upper body of the dress was a fitted corset, encrusted with small crystals, these continued down to the silk taffeta skirt which flowed on the floor. The simple elegance, yet rich in every sense, that was me.

I could feel my soul smile, I felt proud of what I had accomplished in this life, but where there is light, darkness will always follow, ready to extinguish and put it out, this life was no different.

I was a guiding star, touching the hearts of people, leading with love and dedication; I was a pillar of the community, throwing and attending lavish parties, dining with the rich and famous, even royalty welcomed me to their tables. My smile could light up any room and my heart could make anyone feel rich, I touched the lives of men and women, standing up for those who were less able, the vulnerable society.

The Chair of a charity was my role, my commitment to helping others was second to none, there was no one I wouldn't stand up to, if it meant me getting what I wanted for the children. I remember speaking in the great council, fighting for disability rights, asking the members for more money to help invest in these children, going head-to-head with the leaders of the nation, and they loved me, not so much that they bowed down to me, they made me work for it, to prove my worth, but in the end, I always got what the children needed.

I felt every emotion as if it was only yesterday; well to be fair, it wasn't that long ago, and not all turned out great, the pain and the loss of this lifetime stabbed me deep into my heart, I could feel the pain of loss, the loss of a child was the deepest pain to overcome, so I substituted the pain with the passion to help others. On the outside, no one could ever see what I was feeling, but I knew, and money could not fill the void the loss had left.

I was born into a family of wealth and affluence in this lifetime, yet it made no difference to my outcome, as I rebelled with all my might, not unlike my own mother. I ran off to be married to my childhood sweetheart, leaving my family far behind. My husband was a humble man, loving and kind, all he ever wanted was to make me happy. Our marriage was beautiful, building our own house, then starting a family of our own.

I miscarried our first child at six months; it was a girl, then I carried the second child full term only to have a still born child. His body was twisted and taught, his life would have been monstrous in this time, as disabled children were not the norm, and certainly weren't accepted within society. This broke me and our family; I was consumed by grief, my husband found solace in any way but me, worked long hours, leaving me alone with no one but my own demonic thoughts.

So, the happy marriage was no more, unable to move past the grief, I desperately researched into every possible cause of birth defects, miscarriage, and disability. I was grasping at straws, knocking on every door for help and guidance, but there was no one who would or could help console this grief-stricken life. I met many other mothers and fathers who suffered the same fate, consumed by grief and loss. Thus, thrusting me into a role I had never envisaged. My life took on another responsibility, and that was to help others; whilst doing so, I was helping myself. Surrounding myself with other like-minded people who understood me, no words were ever needed, as we understood each other. Our grief and experience connected us in unimaginable ways.

Whilst my husband worked his fingers to the bone, then shared his time with the publicans of the village, I sat alone and researched, writing hundreds of letters to people of science asking for their assistance, in the hope that I may find an answer and live the happily married life I was meant to. I didn't want to walk away from my husband, because despite everything, I still loved him, and I knew deep down, he still loved me too, but grief does strange things, and to be alone was the only option.

Feeling the grief of this past life, and remembering what occurred next, the separation, no longer as one, but I knew that the life was meant to be far more, and I was so very young. It was then that I decided I would do all I could to prevent this happening again in the future. To prevent families from breaking down, to prevent divorce, hurt and pain, and hopefully helping those like me, who despite their attempts to live a beautiful and happy life, ended up living in pain and dismay due to loss.

The wise master in me states-*You must understand the pain of loss to develop wisdom and compassion.*

This was my life's choice this lifetime; I chose loss and my goodness, did I lose, everything I loved I lost, every deep dark fear had become a reality, loss, loneliness, losing two children even before they were born was cruel, yet necessary. It taught me how to fight for what I believed in, no thought for anything else, just my babies which I craved for and those children we had dreamt of having.

Putting my heart and soul into research, I contacted every person I could find, scientist, members of great council, even the nation's leader. After all my efforts, I finally got a break, having the opportunity to speak at the nation's great council. It was a daunting task, but I knew I must do it, as these cases deserved to be recognised. Families needed help after the loss of a child, and leaders needed to recognise the repercussions of not helping them was far greater than investing a few pounds to make some changes. After all, if families succumbed to grief, then they would be unable to work, unable to pay their taxes, unable to participate in raising their other children.

The cost of doing nothing outweighed the small investment I was asking them to contribute. Their contribution would be to invest in guidance, counsellors for all types of loss, including the counselling for those who were expecting healthy children, but were saddened when their children became ill or brain damaged, as they lost part of the child they had planned for. I saw this repeatedly, having a disabled child hurt families in the same way that losing a child did. They couldn't communicate their grief, as this was not the norm; at the end of the day, their child was alive, but not the whole child. Part of the child was missing, the ability to communicate, the ability to move was restricted becoming increasingly dependent of their families to assist. The pain and responsibility weighed heavily on families making them equally as important.

The pain of loss burned deep in soul; my heart felt broken with no means of repair. With all the support I had gained, I created a charity which helped parents like me, finding solutions to the challenges they faced. counsellors who would listen without judgement, securing the foundations of the relationship which once was, but now had changed, changing the family dynamics, giving them a of fighting chance of succeeding and living a life of some normality.

Whilst leading the charity, I had many people whom I worked closely with, confidents who aided me in my journey, they were truly remarkable people. I surrounded myself with those I loved and wanted to succeed; however, there were those who saw what I did as a threat. Those people constantly tried to change the vision I had, suffocating me with their spiteful advice, leading me down paths which I did not wish to take. These people were NOT the people I thought they were, darkness led them, as they tried to infiltrate my energy, hanging to my tails as there was nowhere else for them. Metaphorically, clinging to my dress like insects trying to get to my skin and infect me with the darkness. They wanted control, their egos drove them to take all steps necessary to stop me in my path, and discredit my judgement and my communication. Would these people really stop me in my journey, would they win? I could not see what they did at the time, I had no idea, I was naïve and believed we were all in it together, but that was not the case.

Placing my life on hold for anything else, I absorbed myself into my charity work, my ex-husband had moved on and seemed very happy, and for this I was truly grateful. After four years of being alone, I finally found someone to share the passion with. I met this man at a charity function, sweeping me away with his smooth words and charisma, captivated by his exuberance, I thought this man may be the one who would lift me out of the self-absorbed darkness I was in, as he was adorned by others, I thought he believed in me and the work I was set to do.

My career as a speaker was taking off; I was recognised in every circuit of the rich and wealthy, my partner stood by watching as I out shone his presence. Soon, this became too much; he was eaten by jealousy. He became possessive and dark; his kindness was gone, leaving a bitter taste and distrust, his fanciful ways of wooing the ladies soon became apparent, as he flaunted his antics in front of me.

Again, I ignored what he chose to show me, as it had no relevance in my passion. I was blinkered by my need to help others, my life was OK, so I would let it fly. Then the drinking started, and once home, his envious outbursts shattered my jaw, bruised my ribs, and broke my finger. Unbale to be seen in society like this, I hid from the world, the shame of what was happening, I needed to keep up the appearance of the societal lifestyle.

A short-lived romance. Exhausted and depressed, with a tarnished reputation I had no one to turn to, no friends just acquaintances, but the show must go on. Now, it's back to the party, every person in the room wanted my attention, every person wanted to know how they could help, despite feeling disparaged by the negative news I also felt so proud of what I had achieved; we still had major donors and raised millions of pounds. The extravagant party was a success, finally it was over. I bid goodnight to the final guest, then went up to my room.

My partner was waiting, sitting in darkness. As I opened the door, I heard the clink of a glass, that well-known sound of a bottle hitting a whisky glass. I entered and started to disrobe from my gown, it was heavy, and the zip was difficult to reach, his hands came over and started to undo my zipper, my body was clenched, uncertain of what was to come. His hands stroked my back, then my neck. I turned to say thank you and met his eyes. They were as cold as stone, dark and sultry, then wham, a punch slammed my face. "That's for disrespecting me."

Half-dressed on the floor, grasping at my dress, trying to protect myself, but no use, he was upon me. Ripping my dress from my body, leaving it bare, spitting out hateful words. "How dare you outshine me? You are nothing, you are no one." Barely seeing, as my eyes became slits, my arms fighting him of, my voice screaming, with no sound.

He continued with his venomous words, "You are going to fail, I will make certain you fail, you will be nothing! I already felt like nothing, I remember succumbing to his violence, thinking it will be over soon, then I will leave. His punches came harder and faster; I heard my bone break in my ribs, then my arm, and to end it all my neck. The lights went out, my body was broken on the floor of the hotel room, twitching with its last breaths. I watched as my soul ascended from this ruptured vessel; my soul didn't even stop to look at what had been left behind."

Watching all this as the light I was today was heart wrenching, soul destroying, why did I need to remember this what good was it going to do? What good could I do? Was knowing my past going to help or hinder my future? The person I was in that lifetime wasn't Molly; yes, it was my soul, another name, another era. The lady I was then had left her mark as visions flashed before me, the headlines which hit every news outlet, informing the world of the demise of this wonderful lady who reformed social thoughts, not only through her words but her actions.

The familiar voice spoke. "Her legacy lives on in your time, you know; the world knows of who you were and what you did for vulnerable children and their families."

"What do you mean?"

"Mrs Jonah Humphries changed the way people saw disability, reducing the stigma of disability for children and their families."

Molly: "Disabled children aren't treated that way in today's society."

"Exactly my point, Jonah had a hand in how disability is perceived, her speeches helped form the foundation of every good deed which transpires today."

Light Guide: "You think that people are dark today, but darkness has always been apparent; in fact, in the past the darkness was more visible, as people blatantly harmed others in full view, now it's all hidden. Done behind closed doors, hidden from society, making souls feel like there is nowhere left to turn other than the darkness, that's why the darkness is consuming more than ever."

"In past years, those who were deemed handicapped would be institutionalised, they would be used as Guinea pigs in hospitals, they were tortured without reprimand, Jonah spoke of all these tortures, speaking of her own mental health after the loss of her children; she was a strong woman."

Molly: "Yes, I remember, I also remember her fight with the darkness; again how she wished to die, but she fought anyway."

Light Guide: "Your light is the strongest light I have ever known, yet you doubt your abilities, even though you have been reminded of your past lives, you know where you come from, and what awaits you, still the doubt is there, why is that?"

The light guide spoke the truth, I can remember fragmented parts of my past lives, the people I have been, the achievements and the mistakes made. The memory of those people who had touched my lives, feeling the warmth of their love. The opposite to this is the people I had wronged, the people who had done me harm, forgiveness was hard, and I felt like I was incomplete, like I had part of me missing. I could now see quite clearly that with each life my energy dims a little, leaving me feel lesser than I had the lifetime before.

Light Guide: "Yes, that is why we normally put a cap on how many lifetimes a soul can reincarnate."

Molly: "How many times does a soul normally reincarnate?"

Somehow, I knew that answer, this being 12, so why, how why have I reincarnated so many times?

Light Guide: "You are a master, and you lead by example, you have reincarnated so many times to show man the way, the earth is 4.3 billion years old, and it needed guidance. Each lifetime, your light has dimmed as you have estranged that far from the light, you are becoming more at risk of being unable to remember the light. The only way you can recharge your true energy is to remember your first lifetimes where you were directly connected to source. This will give you the energy you need to complete this final task and save mankind once and for all."

"There is a reason I took you back to your last life first, this was the beginning, the beginning of the end, without this life we cannot mend."

Recognising the eloquent chant of the collective, I asked, "Pardon?"

"Lifetimes give and they take away parts of our light left on display, re-claim your light, and don't lose sight, to make you whole, fulfil your plight."

I could hear the words, but didn't quite understand what it meant. I cannot rectify the past, I cannot change it, how do I fulfil my plight?

We both heard what the Collective said, my light guide was the first to respond. "It sounds like it's a common thing, I have never come across this before, but I suppose it makes sense. I know the lifetimes which have drained me, leaving me feeling weary and unworthy to return home, but then I do, my light is recharged by the collective and off into another lifetime we go. The difficulty in life has always been remembering that we have had past lives, that was always my challenge on earth; I know I have felt like you do; I know what it means to feel whole, do you remember your mission in the past life?"

"This last lifetime was extremely important, cut short by fate and darkness alas, home is awaiting your return, then from you the world will learn."

"OK, so what your saying is that its only my last lifetime which I need to recollect?"

Light Guide: "It's the last lifetime which holds the answer to saving today; it's the last lifetime which can save your family, and it's the mission of the last lifetime which can save the world today, but it's the first lifetime which will give you the energy to fulfil it."

Molly: "Of all the lifetimes I have lived, it had to be the last lifetime which I have to relive, to remember what I could have done differently, what my mission was and why had I chosen loss and return? What is really going on, and why are you choosing to show me my past lives in this life, this is not the norm; this is not how we guide souls. So, why now, what's happening?"

Collective: "Let's cut to the chase, you know how the world was made, how the asteroids collided and created the earth. The dominant asteroid came from a peaceful galaxy, but then combined with other asteroids, then after millions of years, the bacteria from these asteroids and eventually some assistance from the creator gods man was made. Man was initially created by conscious beings who were pure love and light. A war was forged, and an agreement was made, then man was merged with darkness 'ego;' well, now the darkness has decided that enough is enough and they are to consume all. They are tired of the dynamics of earth and want total control. Therefore, in order to save the conscious souls, we need to raise them to another dimension one which they cannot enter into, one made of love and compassion which the darkness cannot reside in."

I could hear the Collectives chant, my Goodness, they like rhymes. "We join as one to make us whole, this discovery was first known, on the return of the first soul, since then we act as one, guiding the souls as we know."

"It makes sense that this could occur, the more lives I have experienced, the more diminished I have become, I wouldn't like to continue my journey to ascension less than complete; if I can fully awaken in this lifetime; then we will guide others to awaken also, and lead them into the Fifth Dimension. I presume that's the dimension you want everyone to go to, but why do I feel that there is something you are not telling me?"

Collective: "This is the only dimension which darkness cannot reside in, so this is what we must do; it will take great power to encourage man to seek his truth. We have tried many times before to encourage man to seek the light. We have shown our presence to man; he just hasn't received it very well. Many guides have been placed on earth as philosophers, wisemen, teachers, scientists, preachers and prophets. Their words have been heard, and many of the spoken words are still used today; man doesn't take too kindly to the word of the light, they want to believe but find it extremely difficult to believe that there is anything but darkness."

"The darkness is far too great and consumes the light with its lies and manipulation, their interpretation of the light's word is muddied and dirtied, so as man is unable to see clearly. We will guide man at a safe distance but having the presence on earth to intervene when needed, lets guide these souls home."

Molly: "OK, I understand that you need my help to guide man towards the light, but why me? There are so many masters, there are so many of us ready to ascend, where are they all and why aren't they talking like they usually do? Today, I have witnessed one past life, but I have had many others, yet it was only this life you had me experience fully, why?"

I could feel the loss within my body, my heart ached, anger raged as I remember the weakness inside, why did I submit my body to such beatings, why was I too scared to stand up to him? So much regret, more regret in this life than any others. Even though my mind was still fragmented, I could feel the past's presence within me, this is another new experience, again one not felt in another life, but why are they doing this and why now?

Collective: "Deep inside, you will dive, the answers within, will then guide."

Collective: "Embrace the lives which did you harm, caused you pain, hurt, erased your calm; the lives it hurts to recall, visit, forgive embrace it all, the light will return if you believe, just do these things to retrieve the memories you need."

Let the journey begin, and with that a smack on the back, a harsh call back to reality. "What ya up to, Molly?" Two wide-eyed boys facing me with cheesy grins on their faces and humour in their voice. Their presence was one of wonder and surprise, love, and compassion.

"Oh, I was just enjoying the peace and quiet, you know."

"Yeh, getting away from your noisy lot, it looked like you were asleep!" They both said in a jovial manner. "Are you coming to the air aid shelters, we are gona make a fire?"

Looking at them, I suddenly remembered that I had lawns to do. "I have to get the lawns done at Bells, I will meet you later, yeh? By the way, what time is it?"

"It's just gone 10 am." They said as they jogged off eager to make mischief.

Oh, bugger, the muck wagon, I told Fin I would help.

Chapter 10

Heading back the way I came, the trees appeared greener, the earth richer and the water stronger; it was like nature was talking to me, reaching out, letting me know they are there. With a sense of contentment, I jogged home, feeling every step, every heartbeat in the rhythm of my body. My body felt like it was finally free from the restriction of fear and worry, maybe now I knew who I was, where I was from and partly why I was here, maybe life would be a little easier to bare.

The conversations I have just partook in seemed like forever, yet it was only 30 minutes in earth time, that was good; I can be absent from reality for longer without raising any suspicion. I needed to start my journey, my soul searching, my remembrance.

Soul searching, is quite a term; it is used all the time by man, as they normally blast it into someone else's face, or scream it in an argument, you need to do some soul searching. Maybe the guides have been trying to guide, now knowing that man is constantly guided by the light guides, I knew that one would be close. They always are, but they cannot interfere in day-to-day life, and for some reason but they don't seem to be reaching man in the way which man can accept, instead man gets frustrated by the tangled messages and hurls them back into the universe as quotes and metaphors.

Now, for the first time, I can see clearly, what the light workers have been trying to do for eons as my past lives become clearer. I can see how I have been guided, or how I have guided my souls in the past, but it is no longer working. The souls are becoming detached, unable to listen, unable to see, feel or accept the signs they are being given. Has man given up? Does man feel worthy to be given these signs, is man ready to be saved? Does man have the ability to awaken to the Fifth Dimension, and is it even possible to take man to the Fifth Dimension with the body still intact? This has never been done before, but I guess, it's never been necessary, so why now, there must be something they are not telling me?

If those questions had been posed to me a few hours earlier, I would have said that I had given up, that I wasn't worthy, I didn't feel worthy to be alive. The fact was I didn't want to be alive; I could see no good in anything, the cup was always half empty, my soul was drowning in negative emotions, I didn't know what to do, or how to save myself. The life I had chosen was slowly killing me. But now, I could see, I had chosen the ultimate test for my final life, if I could save my family, then I could guide the way for the light workers to save the rest.

I was foolish to think I was alone, to think that I was doing this alone, the millions of light workers who stand with us every day, guiding the way, those gentle pushes in the right direction. The change of thought when we want to go one way yet choose another. The feeling in the gut when something is not quite right. The light is always there, it is the animal instinct in human nature, it never leaves us. But can it give itself to the darkness?

I know I have felt the presence of the darkness, that pit in your stomach which swirls like dark muddy water, or the pains in your chest which are as black as the tar they use on the roads, thick and sludgy sticking to you like glue. With no way of relinquishing this sludge, it starts to take over the rest of your body, until the body has no light left, each thought is dark, each memory is negative, you cannot even think of a joyous moment, you are consumed to the darkness to the sadness within.

The light within you continues to fight until the end, but with man becoming more materialistic and wanting more than the light can give, then the darkness is consuming at a faster pace, as man constantly battles with what he doesn't have, spiralling down into the depths of despair and failure. Telling himself those negative thoughts which cause him more harm, reminding himself every minute that he isn't good enough, that he isn't worthy, that he's a failure. But why? Society is paving the way to how man should look, dress, and act, how man should live. These are the control tactics of the darkness, they have found a way to control man, to increase those negative emotions which man finds himself caught up in. It's always been there, but in the past, it was man himself or the newspapers, never has man had so much access to how he should be.

The technology of today has advanced dramatically, with smart technology, mobile phones, computers, oh and the internet, my Goodness, how did we ever survive? But not in our house, we still live in the stone ages, no internet, just 5G. I don't have a mobile phone yet, but Fin has promised me one with his market money. My lack of this technology does cause some jibes at school, but one day all will work out as it should, and at this moment in time I have something far better, I have nature.

As I look around, I finally see the good in the world, as the trees whisper to me in their elegant way, mother nature's communication channel, which is always open for the world to experience, and its free, if only man would stop to listen. Ambling up the final path, the rain drops began to fall; gently they fell like tear drops the drops from a mother's eyes, uninterrupted falling freely, softly, humbly, watering this dry land. A tinge of appreciation ran through this vessel of mine, that's a new feeling for her, she doesn't normally notice these things. Then I realised that vessel was me, I don't normally appreciate these things, really if someone had said appreciate the rain, I would have sniggered and walked away; yet today, I'm old and wise, and I've been here before many times. I think this body is going to be for a rude awakening, but she will be OK.

I welcomed my new self into my body, I was it, and it was me, and we were going to be just fine. We weren't that dissimilar, at least I believed in something more before, and now I know there is more about life than just living. There is a greater purpose to life, we are not placed here unwillingly, we are here on our own personal quest, and now we are on the mission of the creator Gods and Prime, of the Collective to help save man from man, what greater mission could there be?

Never in any lifetimes have I ever felt so empowered by knowledge, well I suppose, I have never known where I came from, so how could I?

"At first, you connected to the source, feel the presence without remorse, the original place from where you were born, the place you are still worshipped and adorn, all is possible if you remember this, better than sinking into the abyss."

My God, they like rhyme, but why rhymes and riddles, what can't they just speak. Never can I remember a lifetime where I felt thankful to be on the earth, yet here I am again, the 360th time, gone full circle, from start to finish. That's the circle of life, my 14-year-old-self giggled at the quote. So many quotes which have been thrown around for decades, which are still used today are guides from the light, we use them but never think to stop how they came about, which wise soul spoke the words.

Walt Disney, he reached man not only through his TV creations but his words.

"The way to start is to quit talking and begin doing." Walt Disney, my mother says this all the time.

The saviour of the world war, with his pragmatic and dry manner stated. *The pessimist sees difficulty in every opportunity. The optimist sees opportunity in every difficulty.*

Sound familiar, no it's not the Collective, it is a world leader, a man who guided this country out of war, only to be penalised and thrown from office, how to be thankful, hey.

A soul which grasped for the world, got thrown in jail and still never gave up on his mission; Mahatma Gandhi spoke some of the wisest words, reaching the hearts of millions.

Where there is love, there is life.

An eye for an eye ends up making the whole world blind.

The weak can never forgive. Forgiveness is the attribute of the strong.

What beautiful words, his words will continue to do good in the world, helping to guide people who are lost, reaching those souls who are unreachable, and upholding those souls who are vulnerable and at risk. The world has been guided since the beginning, but man is too blinded to see it; he is too wrapped up in his own actions to remember.

A raindrop suddenly fell of a leaf right on the end of my nose, a wakeup call, to get a move on, go and help Fin load that muck trailer, then mow those lawns, a promise is a promise. As I started to run, I felt the energy surge through my veins like a turbo charge; honestly, this vessel could go far, I just never realised it before, what a cracking little body, strong and powerful, athletic figure, powerful thighs, great for running. Smiling and filled with joy, I reached the top of the path to find the tractor reversing a muck trailer down the yard. Just in time, or not? I can help Fin load the trailer, then I will go do the gardens.

Forgetting that father was at home, I hurriedly ran down the yard to go help Fin. Instead, I found father standing there watching him. He never got his hands dirty; I don't even know why he is home. Reverting to that 14-year-old girl, forgetting that I was an old soul, I could feel the fear in my gut. My thoughts fraught with what ifs, dark emotions running through my mind, my body tensing as it ground to a halt where he stood.

Come on, Molly, remember who you are; you are a very wise old soul, you never have to fear him again, just walk past with your head held high, no second glance, no second thought, now do it. I could feel his eyes boring into me, daring me to pass, and I did what my soul said. Father stood dumbfounded, stuck for words, and I'm certain I heard him stutter, maybe that's why he ridiculed Fin so much, because Fin was like him. Without any more thought, I went to Fin.

Fin was where I had left him in the calve shed; he was just scraping up the final dregs of the bed, brush in one hand, shovel in another. Looking up, his eyes were reddened as if he had been crying. "Hey, are you OK?"

"Do I look OK?" He said with a grimace. "Where have you been, why didn't you stay around?"

"I went for a walk down the steps, just to clear my head; so much has happened over the last couple of days, I just needed to think."

"Well, you did that at the right time. You know, father's home again, I wished he would go back to work, this just isn't working, I can't be doing with him breathing down my neck."

"Yeh, I know, but there isn't much we can do; we cannot force him to go to work. You know what I think, you should do is to ignore him, pretend like he isn't there."

"Mmm I can imagine him taking that well. Not!"

"Just a thought." My mind shifted back to the sounds of my soul, don't tell him to ignore and don't tell him to challenge; your father is a dark force and needs handling with care, one tip of emotion will make him explode, these souls are extremely volatile. I know I have experienced this before many times, and yet to remember a time where the bright soul has presided over the dark force of the mind. The darkness seems to strengthen man, which makes his presence even more dangerous, then when he hits out which he will, he has the strength to kill.

Remembering my past lifetime, where I was murdered by the hands of the man I thought I loved, he was filled with emotions, anger, rage and worse, jealousy, I see the same traits in this man. In fact, he is very similar. Father has estranged my mother from her wealthy family; he has made her dependent on him alone; she has nowhere to turn. The same type of behaviour which I had experienced in the past, the similarities were resounding. The more I thought about him and how he was, the more I could see the same attributes in father.

"Darkness will always find the light, past lives shared don't lose sight, it is here to take your soul, remember your past and your goal."

The Collective, reminding me that we have had past lives together, thinking back the darkness has been in most lifetimes, but more so in the last six, now, seventh lifetime. The darkness has consumed in most, ending my life with a cut of a blade, or the turn of a neck; the only time the darkness did not take my life was when I chose to have afflictions or creativity, there was something about those lives that it did not reign as I died of natural causes, painful natural causes, but natural all the same.

In recollection of the past, I turned to Fin. "Don't worry, we will find a way to overcome father, he's not that clever, we will be OK." There is one thing different in this life than in all the others; this life I could remember, I can remember who I was, what I had done, but most of all, what I had learnt, and that had to count for something.

With that comment, Fin smiled and continued to finish his work. The farmer unhooked the trailer and left it at the side of the muck pile, ready to be loaded. It's the twenty-first century and majority of farmers have tractors to do this work, but not father; he never makes life too easy, our home, our farm is like stepping back in time, when all the world is moving forward, our lives are treading on days gone by, living in the past, a place and tradition which father was accustomed to.

I looked around and sure enough, father had disappeared; his car had gone, no doubt to do some very important business, as he will say to justify his actions, but 'really' he just wanted to get out of work. This man is lazy, bone idle, he doesn't have a working day in his body, a bit like Arty, he is lazy, takes after father, like two peas in a pod.

It's funny how souls take on traits of those they are born to, they have no previous commonality with these people, yet they start to act and sound like them. Throughout my lifetimes, I can recall the times where I have been a double of the person I was born to. Amused by this thought, I set to work helping Fin load the trailer. Fin was loading his fork with huge amounts of muck and throwing it like it was a sweet paper, for such a small boy, he has a mighty arm. Whereas I was loading my fork just enough, so as none would fall and land on top of my head.

Throwing muck onto a muck trailer is no easy feat, especially when the trailer was at least one foot taller than you. This little body I was in had an unfair disadvantage, her small stature had no chance of averting muck on the head, no matter how much muck she placed on the fork. Helping her out a bit at this time would be good; in an instant Molly started to throw the muck high in front of her, instead of over the head, making it less likely to fall on her angelic locks.

Recognising this change in throw, Fin said, "It's about time you threw like a man, with a throw like that we will have this trailer loaded in no time." With a chuckle, we both continued to load the trailer, in rhythm with each other's throw. In a race of time to get done, so as we could do what?

Well, I needed to mow the lawns for Bell and Mrs F. I told Fin what Matt and Ste were up to mischief in the air aide shelters, so maybe he would join them.

But really, I wanted time alone to figure out how I was going to remember my past lives and reconnect to my first lifetime. How the hell was I going to do that? The soul missions are set prior to birth, then we normally spend a lifetime trying to work out why we are here, so where did I even start? The rhythm of throwing the muck was cascading my thoughts all over the place, the lifetimes I had lived, the hurt and pain I had felt, the worry I have experienced in lifetimes, and for what? Now, I realise that worry has no place in life, there is no point in worrying about anything, as it only attracts more of what you think about.

In past lives, I have worried about everything, and true enough, what I have worried about has manifested.

Worried about being dependent, then had a relationship where the man alienated all my friends and family, making me alone, making me feel worthless. With only him to depend on, making me dependent, but really was it him? I had free choice, I had free will, yet I allowed this to happen. I could see what was happening, yet I did nothing to stop it, nothing to correct him, I put up no fight, why? Fear, that if I challenged him, he would leave, and I would have no one.

Wow the realisation of what my vessels mind had created in those lifetimes, or was it the vessel. I am the soul, I am the thought, the consciousness, which part of us holds the darkness. Is it the host are they born with darkness in the DNA or is it me? Is it the soul? I listened to the guiding words of my inner soul as it answered with precision and wisdom.

Soul: "The soul controls the heart, and the ego controls the mind. These two are in constant conflict, the heart will say go left, and the mind will say go right, you know the heart to be true, but the ego is also very powerful, so which one do you listen to? The subtle whispers of the heart/soul or the pushy ego/mind? The ego wins until you finally awaken to the realisation of what you are doing to yourself. No one in the world can hurt you unless you let them, a snide comment which the ego would take straight to the heart, would hurt for days, but what would happen if you just let it go?"

Acceptance is something that isn't natural to man, as they always find some way to defy, or blame, or make it about them. What if every man didn't take things to heart as much; what if man just accepted that a friend was in a bad mood, and ranting, not to you, but to themselves; it is not personal. What if man just listened, accepted, and then moved on? What would the picture look like then? Then man would be mindful; he would be aware of what his mind is thinking; how the man reacts and how the mind causes unnecessary pain on the human body.

Maybe if man was able to become more mindful, then he would be at one with himself; heart and mind in balance. Paying attention to his actions, to his feelings and emotions, his ability to recognise good and bad feelings. I've never been the type of soul that uses the word bad; in fact, I don't particularly think that anything is bad, just different. So, let me rephrase that, man could develop the ability to recognise what feels good, and what makes him feel less than good. The feeling of less than good can then be embraced and welcomed the same as the good feeling, making each feeling equal. Drawing the balance between emotions, accepting that each has its place, and not punishing yourself for how you feel, but just accepting it.

This is all a bit deep, I know, but throughout lives, I have allowed others to influence how I think, how I feel, how I act, despite which vessel I was in. Now in this time of awakening and realisation, I know this life needs to be different; I need to awaken fully to the possibility of change. The great leaders of this world have paved the way, their words resonate with man, their wisdom carries us on our daily journeys.

Buddha said, *Our life is shaped by our mind, for we become what we think.*

No truer words have been spoken, yet we do not listen. Man is always one step ahead, never in the moment, rarely in the present, so what does that mean for man, what is he learning, if he never stops to connect? Connect to the earth and to himself. Man is not living, he is existing, fulfilling a task then moving on; life is just one huge task, with no real end and no apparent beginning.

Chapter 11

The most serene life I can recollect was as a monk; one of my first lives before the common era. Times were no different than they are today, even though, there were less people, conflict was still present. The monks resided in the Indo kingdoms, , the province was ruled by more than thirty kings, each conflicting with the other. There were also many religions, each grasping for the control of the other.

However, the external world did not penetrate the daily living of a monk. The life we led was peaceful, at one with me and with nature, we tended the lands, and prayed. Initial emotion to this remembrance of life was one of awe and inspiration, but in realisation, I'm not sure. The life wasn't without its downfalls; after all, I was thrown in a camp left by a feared ruler who wanted only one religion to preside. He didn't favour the Buddhist practices and decided to place his wrath on all those who did. Death and destruction lay in his wake.

Nonetheless, my time as a monk taught me self-preservation of the mind, how to control the mind. Erm, I don't like the word control, so I will rephrase it, how to accept the mind, that's better. Talking to myself is the first sign of a crazy person, self-realisation, sweetie; you don't have to think of it as talking to yourself, but maybe accepting and welcoming an old friend into your life. You are 14 years old, there is so much I can teach you, listen and feel. Your soul is now awake, I reside in your body, your mind will think and feel what I feel in some ways, but in others, the mind will rebel, as the mind also has ego, and ego always tries to rule, the key is to find balance.

Soul: "I know, this is strange, but we need to be as one, I will teach you, my life as Buddha I taught many how to find and hold peace. The balance of oneness resides in every man, the acceptance of body, mind, and soul. You too can learn this. You too may have no choice but to learn it, never before has the soul been disclosed to its vessel."

Molly: "I know that this is my soul talking the inner words, it feels strange to have a conversation within, even though I have these conversations all the time; something now feels different the presence is stronger and more willed. In the past, my heart would ache as I dreamt of a better life, but my mind would always win. Putting me in my societal place, reminding me that I'm not good enough, reminding me constantly that I am not worthy of love. Leaving emptiness, anxiety, the inability to breath, making me long for death, for it all to end. So, if it means sounding like a crazy person, or losing to my dark thoughts, then I will go with the soul, hopefully it will drown out the pain which I feel."

Soul: "Don't be disillusioned; just because you are accepting your soul as part of you doesn't mean that you will always have peace and serenity. My past lives have been somewhat traumatic, and you will have a ring side seat. You will experience what I have in my past lives, but it may give you insight to the difficulties I have encountered, and successes I have been part of. This will be no easy deed; you know that the mind and the soul don't work in complete harmony; the mind is partly the ego. The part of you which always wants more, the part of you which keeps you a controlled manner, letting you believe you're not good enough. The soul seems to join along for the ride, then awakens when they are older, but many times when the soul awakens, they are too old or too scared to do anything. They then stay lost in lives which they don't belong, unable to achieve their life's purpose."

Molly: "Well, that's not going to be me; I mean us, we are going to succeed, and we are gona kick ass in this lifetime, then you can ascend, and I will return to the earth, where I will be with what I love, nature."

Soul: "Sounds like a plan. We will give it a go, but you must understand, there have been very few lifetimes where I have experienced true peace; even as a Buddhist, there were those who feared the tradition. Those who didn't understand, so with that they waged a war against it, nearly defeating it to extinction. We were cast aside, but even during the peaceful times, there is always war. The war within, the war without. War has been present from the start of recorded time, one man's fear of loss can create powerful allies, powerful weapons and powerful armies. Its man's fear which creates destruction, yet it is man's courage which creates peace, but man has yet to awaken to this."

"Take a high school bully; he pushes a kid around, ridicules him and makes him scared to go to school. Then one day, another kid sees this, and goes over, standing up to the bully, making him back of, the bully slopes away sniggering. Who is the most courageous?"

Molly: "Well, the kid who stuck up to him. I see what you mean, but that's life."

Soul: "Yes, it is, but we need more people to stand up to the bullies; we need more courageous souls."

Me: "Have you ever experienced a life without war? Has there ever been a peaceful leader?"

Soul: "Yes, a long time ago, there was a place called the Dusia Civilisation; life there was beautiful, everyone as equals, people living together, helping each other, no famine no war, no rulers, well, not on the earth."

"What do you mean?"

"The awakening was a slow process, remembering past lives was like awakening from a coma and re-learning how to function. The lifetimes which I recall were peaceful had assistance and guidance from another realm, a realm which I was originally born from, but I have had so many lives on earth, my thoughts of home are distorted. However, I do remember their presence, the light, the love, the energy."

Soul: "Their guidance was at times of extreme importance to mankind, yet mankind will still not connect the dots, the possibility of other realms visiting the earth, assisting man to become all he can, guiding him through construction, science, and knowledge, through the love. Love resides in everyone, if man can do what he loves, then peace will follow; this was the world of the realm. When man has been left to his own devices, death and destruction have always been part and parcel. Few rulers have been left to rule in peace, as their peace has been deemed as being a sign of weakness, thrusting them into battles they did not want and could not win."

Soul: "Yet when interaction has occurred then this was time for peace, for growth, for development. It's as if they were giving man the tools to build a greater world, but instead man fears the changes, fears the difference, and uses the technological advances for war. They think that justifying it with the word defence is applaudable, how many times do they use these defence weapons to attack? They are too naïve to see that they can use the technology to advance life on earth, using it to cleanse the atmosphere, using it to help the planet. They don't do that; they use the technology to make money, to have more, consumed by greed, ignoring the needs of their own people."

Thrown back into a life where people were starving, I was one of them. The hunger in my stomach, the dryness of my mouth as I yearned for water and food. Set in a crowded place, at the side of a huge palace, hundreds of bodies climbing around the floor, each as hungry and thirsty as the other. Their cries harmonised. As I lay on the floor, I could see the wheels of cars going into the huge gates. Looking across, I could see people holding onto railings, screaming for food and water, yet no one was coming. At the other side of the railings, looked like a party. Rich people were strolling about in refined clothes, they were drinking and eating, whilst we were at the gates crying for food.

As I felt the anger well up, I realised that in that lifetime, I was only a child, maybe two years old. My frail body was skin and bone, my mother by my side crying as my body deteriorated. When was this, I couldn't recollect this lifetime, where was it? Insane flashes of cruelty, where power ruled supreme. The mighty voice boomed across the plane, Mothers who bore more than one, must now pay the price. The rules are here to be obeyed, abide by them, or watch your child die. Again, the lifetime was set in the east, the need for control always appears to be more prominent here. The one child rule, if women had more than one, then the child would have to die.

Baby girls were left by roadsides or worse, they were thrown away like trash. This is the epitome of man's ego. One man's need for the ultimate control, to control human nature, to control the birth of souls. The male species is less inclined to seek the truth of the soul, hence why we choose the female species prior to ascension; this species appears to be less likely to atone to the darkness, although it does still occur. My feeble infantile body gave up the fight and left for the light. I still recall the cries its mother made, those haunting wails of pain and hurt.

Ouch. A thud on top of my head, straw covering my eyes, and the weight on my head. Flipping heck, the muck fork had slipped, landing a great big pile of dung on my head. Fin stood there laughing, and soon enough, I laughed along. The muck trailer was loaded high with pig, cow, and chicken dung; we had done it. My body was wet with sweat, my head crammed with the past lives of my soul. Visions which cannot be unseen; visions which I accept will help me be a stronger, more compassionate person. But for now, I need a drink, and a shower. The shower part is out of the question, as the fire isn't lit, so there will be no hot water, I will have to wait until later. I'm 14 years old, no one is gona bother if I smell a bit. Giggling, we head up to the house, there's still water in the taps, so that is OK.

As we open the farm gate before the house, we both notice father's car is on the drive again. Looking at each other, we continue to walk in anticipation of what may lie ahead. The foul mouth of a scared man, mother standing there with her bags packed, father grasping at her, instructing her to stay with him. Threats of all sorts, not least the threats of her children, oh yes, he went there. I will take my life; I will take them too! As we walked closer, mothers' eyes widened, her eyes urging us to run. I could feel my blood boil, the energy surged within me. No more, no more lives of being pushed around, being dominated by man. There was going to be a shift.

Taking my stance, watching father's actions, his frantic fight to say what was needed to keep mother in her place. But I wonder, what he would do if someone stood up to him. With that thought, I walked over to him, and said, "Do it, take my life." He stood dumbstruck, unable to say anything; this lazy weak man who ruled his home with threats and manipulation, due to his fear of losing such a beautiful lady. I don't even know why she chose him; she could have done so much better; she was beautiful, he looked like a slimy weasel. Thinking all of this whilst I stared at him, passing my energy on to him, showing him what I felt, what I knew.

Watching him squirm in front of me, I challenged him again, I even goaded him. "Come on, you can do it, just click my neck, I'm tiny, turn out the lights, then she will stay, if you don't, you won't lay another hand on her ever again." I could see his frustration, he wanted to lash out, but he was a coward; he couldn't show anyone his dominant side, well other than mother. "You use your fists to keep he in her place; you couldn't possibly keep someone like her without some kind of threat." His face reddened with anger, my words were having an impact, but it wasn't me that was going to pay, it was mother. "Don't think for one minute that we don't know what you do, you're a coward! Go, mother, get out of here, you deserve better, we will be OK." As my elder soul, these are the words I said, but the 14-year-old me was crying inside as she saw her mother climb into a neighbour's car and leave.

Fin turned to me. "Why did you just do that, why did you make her go? She would have stayed, she always stayed." I was shocked by his outburst; for the first time in this rotten life, I had done something that no one else had dared, I had stood up to father, but at what cost? As an old soul, I knew the costs, mother would certainly pay, if she ever came back which I'm sure she would. Looking at Fin as he cried, I answered. "I'm sorry, Fin, but someone had to stand up to father." But Fin was having none of it. I have never seen him so cross; normally he is my go-to guy, the one who makes me laugh, the one who seems to laugh at the world. But for the first time, I see another side to him, the struggle he is having with his inner conflict, his heart and mind thrashing it out.

"I wished I never told you that father beat mother, now they both know, and they will have someone to blame, it's always me, I'm the one father is going to take this out on. God, I wished I wasn't here, I hate this life!" Wow, this explosion of honesty drew me back, my feelings, my emotions, I wasn't alone, I wasn't the only one who wanted it all to end. Fin paced anxiously on the drive, father had disappeared again, nowhere to be seen and mother was in the next lane with a family friend. Observing Fin was heart breaking; this beautiful soul in so much pain, I awaited his next outburst. "I'm sorry, Fin, I'm just tired of living in fear, I'm tired of bullies and I too am tired of this life." Fin's face softened, the anxiety easing as his breathing became more regular. "What now? No mother, a father who's handy with his fists, brothers who constantly tells me I ain't good enough, and wants to send me back to children's home and another who likes to use me as their punch bag."

His words scorched with every letter; this life I have chosen is simple on the exterior, but underneath the layers, Fin was not exaggerating. It was a hell of a life for a young child, never mind an old soul, and If I can bring this vessel out of this environment sane, then it will be an achievement. Fin spoke the truth, his perception of this life was clear, but where was it going to lead him. Was he going to rebel against the darkness, which was looming, and blind it with the light which shone within him? Something told me that he had the ability to do both. Fin was an old soul, he had been here many times, I could feel his energy as it poured out of him.

His words were manic, as he ranted like he had lost his mind, but his speech and breathing were clear, so he wasn't panicked, his words were frenzied making no sense. As concern arose "Fin, are you OK, what are you saying?" The look of calmness on his face caused even more concern; he looked fine, yet his words were chaos, and made no sense at all. "I am fine, Molly, nothing to concern yourself with. You made your stance, showed your hand, now let's move on, draw a line in the sand." The words made me shudder. I have heard that line before, *draw a line in the sand*. In fact, I heard that saying many times, in many lives, and it's never been good, it's the Alamo all over again, a challenge a dare to cross.

I watch him move calmly forward, as if he is possessed by another. Could it be, has the darkness taken him? It's more likely to have taken father than Fin. Molly thinks about it, the darkness is more prone to taking the young as they are more susceptible to their suggestion and manipulation. I knew this to be true due to the lives I have lived; I have seen children turn on their own parents, wipe out their whole families, as the darkness has taunted them into doing their bidding, wiping out any chance of light in the children's lives, ensuring they are dependent on the darkness.

Don't get me wrong. I understand the frustration when children witness adults doing shocking things, like beating their mother, or worse messing with their children. I understand that children can retaliate, but the darkness doesn't ask for it in retaliation, they ask for it because they can. The darkness likes to know how much of a hold they have on man, to keep him in check, and in every lifetime, dark keeps with dark; therefore they will and do always stand by the side of another dark soul. The darkness has a way of attracting dark and redacting any light which comes their way, yet they can trick light to their smoothness and animalistic attraction. We all know the saying when a person is attracted to a bad boy, excitement, exhilaration, it feeds the darkness within.

For instance, have you ever entered a room and felt a negative energy? You scope the room, and see smiling happy faces, then you see, that one person who makes you shudder, you don't know why, but you take an instant dislike to them. Later in the evening, you are introduced to them by a mutual friend, the person opposite you is smiling and charming, but your gut is screaming get away, stay away, you really do not want to get to know this person. The charms of the person will try to bowl you over, it's at this point in life when you must listen to your body, listen to what it is saying and get out of there.

My gut is screaming right now, my brother Fin, the one who makes me laugh, makes me feel safe, is my confident, has changed. I have never felt any negative energy from him before, I have never seen him look at father in that way before, but I guess, we have never had our mother walk out on us before, well not with bags anyway. I just couldn't grasp why he was so angry at me standing up to father, or why he would want to protect him; why when only the other day father was raging at Fin and wanted to take his earnings from the cattle market for his own. Why would Fin even care what father thinks? I understand Fin's concern for mother, and why she left; after all, he is the one that hears the nightly beatings, he is the one who has no choice but to listen. So, why oh, why would he have a look of concern for father, why would he want to protect him?

I watched Fin as he mooched down the lane, his head hung low, his shoulders sagged, his beautiful vibrant energy was dominated by dark clouds of black and purple. The further away he got, the more I could see what was happening, the aura around his body was vivid blue, bright and flamboyant, but surrounding it was the dark mist, as it tried to stifle the colour, suffocating its brightness with its deep depressed manner. I wished I could wave a wand, and all be back to normal, well whatever that is.

Chapter 12

The last few days have been traumatic, to say the least, what with father and his brother Jimmy, I still don't know what will become of that and what will become of Fin? Father is at home more, which is never good, as bad things happen when he is around. Not bad as in life threatening, it's just an energy shift; everyone seems grumpier, snappier, as though they are trying too hard, but not being recognised for it. I know that makes no sense, but I know when I try too hard, or I am really focused on doing the very best, then I have no patience for anyone or anything else, thus meaning I am snappy, hence the reason why I believe the energy changes so much when father is around; they are either scared of him, or trying to impress him, either way, it's not good.

I have never experienced this change in Fin before, I haven't seen him react in this manner. To see his energy being absorbed so rapidly was unprecedented. In all my lifetimes, I cannot remember a time where a soul has been taken in this manner. The energy change occurs over time, months, years, yet today, it was minutes. There can only be one explanation, the darkness is becoming more powerful, or it has a way of masking its identity. I have always been able to read energy, feel energy, to know whether it is positive or negative, but this lifetime is obviously different, as I am awake and can see the energy. Seeing energy is far more advantageous than feeling, and its beautiful, until it's not.

Thinking whilst watching my brother walk ahead, seeing his forever changing energy, watching the colours intermingle, dark with light, as they battle for the ultimate power. Which one was going to conquer, and which would submit? But I couldn't wait around to find out, as I had made a promise to mow Bell's lawn. Fin went left and I broke right. I knew where he was going, he was going to see mother, but his energy wasn't right, how would that effect mother? Worry was not going to help, he needed to do what he needed to do; I was not to intervene, it was not my path.

I clicked the gate latch and went to knock on the back door when the door opened. The entrance hall was illuminated with bright white mist. I had seen this before in Havenmoor, but why was it here? They have made me aware. I knew what I needed to do. I needed to complete the soul searching, so what now, I didn't have time for their games. I entered the house filled with positive energy, radiating through every crevice, raising my vibration, and easing my frustration. Welcoming the calmness, I called for Bell, but no answer. I entered the pantry and there she stood in all her glory, the ultimate energy source, one of purity and love.

The kindness on her elderly face was dazzling, the energy in her bright green eyes vibrated with a loving energy and acceptance as she welcomed me in. "Hello, Master." Her voice greeted me, unbeknown to me, Bell was a light worker, and she knew it. "Bell, how?" I knew Bell had a special connection to me, and obviously, I knew she would return to the light, as she was a positive soul and kept away from the darkness, but I didn't realise that she was awake. I should have known, it was naive of me to think that I was alone, the Collective are called the Collective because of one reason- they work better together.

I wonder how many light workers have been awakened, just as Bell answered. "There are 100 Guardians of light who are working with the hundreds of light workers/light guides to awaken the masters here on earth. Masters have chosen to come to earth at this time, to save man from man, but never has a master been awake during this process. That's why they are masters; they normally can link to the source and fulfil their mission regardless. However, the masters have resided here for many lives, diluting their ability to link to source, leaving them susceptible to the dark forces. Thus, the awakening. Masters must then work with the vessel, remember the past lives, then transition to the new dimension." Bell spoke, even her voice was calming. "Thank you, Bell."

"So, here we are on this earth plane, ready to save the world." I said in a sarcastic manner, the self-doubt seeping back in, as I recalled Fin's energy being absorbed by the darkness right before my eyes. The darkness is becoming brazen, showing itself in that manner. The anger was seeping out of me like a sieve, my energy which had been lifted was dimming due to the emotions I felt for my brother, the love the concern, yet with this came negative energy, anger, frustration, bitterness, and self-blame, loathing even. He was going through a terrible time, and I was stood here with my radiant light worker, how was that fair?

"Molly." Bell's voice called out, "You must let go of the vessel, it's the vessel that ties you to the emotion, ties you to the earth brother." And with that, my energy dispersed and my emotions balanced. I was out of my mind, or so they say. The term out of your mind is quite innate, as it suggests that you are crazy or frantic. The books I have read, the term is used, "He was out of his mind with worry." If only they knew what the term out of the mind means? For me, it means, to be out of my mind is to be in control. Why has no one ever thought of it that way? Even Buddha was out of his mind most of the time, rarely did his mind touch the heart, yet man still cannot relate.

Bell's energy was vibrating, pulsating to arhythmical beat. The beat was a thud ever few seconds. Looking around, I could not see where it was coming from, but I felt it, the noise vibrated through the energy field causing it to ripple, the more it rippled, the bigger the field got. It was simply beautiful, like a calm ocean lapping at the sand, tickling its granules, then retracting, but each time it came into shore, it would come further and further, until it covered the entire shore with its surge of power and energy, replenishing the sand beneath.

Bell's voice called me back, "Master, we await you." Lost in my own thoughts and memories I returned to the present, seeing Bell's energy was a swift reminder of what was, what is and what will always be. Bell was the link to mother nature, her stunning colours were unmistakable, soft pink hues, with ripples of earths colours of green, yellow, brown, blue, violets, the true rainbow energy. The joyful beat which Bell's energy danced to was that of something or somewhere I recognised, but I cannot recall. Was it mother nature, the tender thrumming of the earth's core.

I felt at home, warmed by the love of my light worker. "I believe we have a job to do." I finally said. The pulsating energy lifted me up, leaving my vessel and the worries of my brother behind. I had a job to do, and I was going to do it. The conscious mind was awakened, the voices softly mumbling with a child-like excitement, my thoughts cleared, and we all joined together, the light emanated around the world as the light workers and masters joined here on earth for the first time. The Guardians of Light are a select few of the Collective; they are normally guiding from an energy form and rarely visit earth in full human form; however, times are changing which are detrimental to mother earth and mankind, hence the need to show themselves.

I had never known the Collective to demonstrate their presence on earth in this manner, they normally send masters as preachers, or prophets, the softy approach is their normal form, but rarely has the conscious soul been awake during a lifetime, it is not normal procedure to remember past lifetimes. As the guardians, light workers and masters, joined here on earth, each shared their earth lives with the Collective, then released it to the universal energy. It was astounding how many souls were unhappy, how many lived despondent lives, a sad existence. Is this what life on earth has emaciated to? The Collective's energy surged and grew with the drumming of mother's beat, the ripple began, it broadcast around the world, the largest antenna in the world was man.

Would man respond? Would man feel it, or is he too far gone? The energy of the universe is lifted, giving man time to accept and absorb his emotions, and see the light. This was a far cry from what mother would have chosen, mother would have sent an earthquake, or tsunami. Oh, yes, she's already done all of that, and man failed to stay awake.

What an impossible task man has got, even if he knew of all of this, would it change anything? Life on earth is no easy achievement; life on earth is the ultimate challenge, where there is little happiness, laughter, or freedom. Don't get me wrong, man has the freedom to do what he likes, but he doesn't, because he is constantly held back because of the world's depiction of how he should be, how he should act. Man lives a life of fear; in fact, to be harsh, man doesn't live, man is part of an experiment to see how the species would live in a controlled environment, but this isn't how it was meant to be.

Man was created by the earth though in the eyes of the Creator Gods and the Prime Creator; earth was meant to be the inter galactic trade system and would house the cosmic library of consciousness, but this created great wars in the galaxy which the Prime Creator and his allies, the creator Gods lost, and new Gods regained. The new Gods were specialist in DNA and genetic sequencing, technology and mind control. Upon defeat, the Prime Creator agreed to surrender to man, but with one rule, no Gods were allowed to directly communicate with man. However, the Egoiks were not in agreement, as they wanted their DNA within the creation; it was an unfair disadvantage that man was made in the image of the Prime Creator and his Creator Gods, they must also have part of the Egoik species within them.

The Prime Creator species were meant to be creators; they were extensions of themselves, and man still has his lineage yet is unable to use it, but the light workers have a way of redesigning the human DNA; we have a plan to save man from himself. Mother earth has witnessed all this upheaval, she has tried her best to cleanse man through the structures of food, climate, and sustainability, but each time she is close, man is drawn back into the claws of darkness, and the darkness rules, mother is now unable to reset, as they now control the weather which controls the planet.

As we all joined together, the vibration of the Collective was all powerful, surging around the world, awakening the old souls who had chosen this mission, the indigo children, angels, other galactic beings, and masters alike. This is just the beginning; the results would only be known in the coming weeks, maybe years in earth time. My soul was in sync with the earth souls, not the Collective at Havenmoor. I could see, hear, feel their presence, the colourful energy, swirling around like a typhoon, sweeping up all the negative and spitting it out.

The power source fed from mother earth, the vibration of earth was becoming more and more dominant, flooding out all negative thoughts and emotions. Then, boom, the oneness was shattered, the vibration had ceased, the connection was lost. I'm certain that wasn't meant to happen. I looked over to Bell, her energy was still vibrant, but no longer radiating like it had been before. "What has happened? Bell?" She wasn't answering, I was still connected to her, I could sense her, it was as if she was trying to communicate but couldn't. I stayed with her for a while longer, the rest of the Collective were in dire straits, the unknown was upon us, did we fail? "No, we did not fail." Bell's voice bellowed through the Collective. "The joint task was a success, many of the light workers and masters have awoken; it's just going to be a matter of time and patience now before we will know the results."

"So, what does this mean? Is the task here on earth done, can we continue with our personal journeys?" Questions were flooding in from all of the volunteered souls, as uncertainty was writhe, what had we actually done, what was the point of the task?

Me: "Will those who have been awoken be able to communicate with us?"

Me: "What is the point in awakening them?"

Me: "Will they know they have been awakened?"

So many questions. Bell answered in her dignified manner. "The task was done in this way to see if man could respond to our presence. We have tried it many times with just one person, but we felt more were required, the human vessel is not able to transmit in the way it was designed, so we felt if more pure souls were able to participate, then the vibration would be more powerful. Those who have been awoken will not be able to communicate with us in the way that we do, but you will be able to better sense them; they will be able to ask questions and you will hear, but they may not hear the reply as their vibration is not yet strong enough to accept it."

My God, this is complicated, my thought zoomed through me as if I was back in my vessel; too late, everyone heard it. Companionship and comradery were all around me, agreeing in unison. As if life on earth isn't challenging enough, now there are new rules, more things to take on board.

Bell's voice was soft and gentle, "It's not complicated, it's as simple as time. We did this joint task for two reasons; one, to let you know, you're not alone, and you have always got each other to communicate with, and two, to make it easier for you to recognize the positive souls to better safeguard you against the negative and the darkness."

Me: "Well, put it like that, it is simple."

Bell: "In time, you will soon start to behave like the master you are, you will let go of the ego, sarcasm, the little quips which make you think, make you feel better; you will be at peace and will no longer let emotion drive you."

Me: "Now, that sounds like something I definitely welcome. I feel tired of the way I act as a human, but the habit does follow me into the source. Will I really be able to manage it better, will I ever be at peace?"

And with that thought, my eyes opened and here I was back in the vessel known as Molly. Bell's eyes were watching me as I awoke, her reassuring presence making me feel safe and loved.

"Hello," she said. I smiled in a reply, but my heart was still aching, my body shaking because of what I had seen Fin do. I was 14 again and felt afraid. It didn't matter what happened to me in the world of the Collective; it was the life within the vessel I was more concerned about.

"Molly, you are a brave soul, you are an elder and have experienced a universal life span. Please embrace your lives, don't make what you have been through pointless, or meaningless; your lives matter, you are the master of masters, there is no one higher, there is no one mightier on this earth at this time." I knew what she said, but could it be true, the emotions within the vessel were powerful and were drawing me into the abyss, I didn't know how to escape.

I recall some of my past lives, but never in any of my lives had I ever felt this low, this depressed, this suicidal. This lifetime is different, I don't know whether it's me, the vessel, the time, or that the darkness is becoming more powerful. I'm not certain what is real and what is make believe. What if I am just making all of this up my head? What if I am not a master? What if the lives I'm recalling weren't real either? What does it all mean?

I was angry. I wanted to scream. I wanted to shout. I wanted to blind myself so as I never saw myself again. I felt like I was going insane, it was all too much; it had all occurred in three days, maybe I was just mad. I had received one too many cracks around the head and I had brain damage, my mind was playing tricks on me. The self-doubt devoured me, and the tears fell, I wept like a baby, my body shaking viciously, I couldn't catch my breath, and I didn't know what to do, think or feel.

Bell's arms wrapped around me. The warmth of her love soothed my emotions, and calmed my body. Her touch needed no words; I could just feel her, the energy radiated through me filling my vessel with positive energy, seeking out every negative patch and replacing it with beautiful light. Her belief and devotion was unmistakable.

"Sweet Molly, you are the strongest soul I know, your commitment to the cause has never faltered. You are here because you want to be, because you believe in man's existence. You are a leader of the new age, and you can do this." What did she mean? My vessel could not take in the words she spoke; I could feel her love and belief and deep inside my soul, I knew her words were the truth, but my mind was playing tricks on me? How could I overcome this self-doubt?

"You use the light within, you must absorb the darkness, merge with it, accept it, only then will you disempower it's hold over the vessel. The darkness is within your DNA."

"How is that even possible? How can the darkness have such a grasp on my vessel? I was in control of me, my thoughts are my own, my feelings are my own, how do I break free?"

"Use the light, use the energy, you must feel it somewhere, you must be able to tap into the source energy." I could only feel Bell's energy, it was feeding me; I was absorbing it like a sponge, taking more and more, but I was unable to feel my own light, I could only feel the pain in my heart. My heart was heavy, there was no light there, there was no love, just pain, worry and fear; it felt like a led weight in my body, this is where my light should be. I knew this, but how could I open my heart, how could I feel any love, when all as I felt was fear.

I was inconsolable, I just wanted it to end, I wanted to curl in a ball and be left to return to the earth, was that even a choice now. "That is not a choice, Molly, you have love in your heart. You have light, it's there, you must connect to it, feel what you once felt, remember where you came from, feel the love of home." Home, that was a fearful word. How was I able to return home? My mother had left, I had challenged my father, my siblings reviled me, I was fourteen. What was I meant to do?

"Your mother loves you; she needs you to be strong. Fin needs you to guide him to the light. Your father can no longer be saved, he has given himself to the darkness, but there is hope for the rest."

Mother earth: "Molly, listen to me. You are my family; you are my energy. I believe in you and all you do; you have the strength to do this; you can do this. You must control your vessel, control the emotions within, breathe."

The positive words resonated with my soul. Who was it? The sound was unknown to me. I had never heard this voice before. How to control the vessel to which I was born? She wasn't ready, her body was limp, all hope was gone, she had no fight. How could I regain control of something which was incapable to listen? "She can hear you, her body has gone into shock, but she will regain consciousness and at that time, you will be waiting, with strength and courage, just be patient."

It felt like my vessel had got her wish, she was dying, her heart was darkened, there was no beat, her body had given up the fight, all hope was gone. "Just be patient, awakening can be traumatic, and normally takes a lifetime; even then the vessel has never fully awakened. Remember, this is the first time a vessel has truly awakened, she has to be in line with you, with your memories, with your past."

"What has happened over the last few days has taken its toll, it's been too much information for the vessel to manage, but it must happen, we cannot wait much longer, man needs to be led into the Fifth Dimension."

Gasping for breath, reaching out for fresh air, Bell holding my vessel with all her might, whilst my vessel regained consciousness. Fear rippled through me, the vessel was remembering my past lives, remembering me, I was her soul. She lay there still in Bell's arms, accepting her energetic force. Slowly, her eyes opened and through them, she could see a new world, her heart was melting, accepting the light which filled her, the fear, depression, and anxiety dispersing, and she knew she would be OK, she wasn't alone.

The Collective soon joined in the awakening, all the vessels had awakened at the same time, each one was now fully awakened into the age of the light, they were ready to absorb the darkness in full force. "Molly, its OK." Bell's hand was slowly stroking my head, the light years were passing through, my eyes opened to the light of the room, making me blink uncontrollably. I was here, whole, and intact; my vessel was in sync and knew the task at hand, Bell was my saviour. "Thank you." I said finally.

Bell's gaze was seductive and beautiful. "You've been through quite a journey. We weren't sure how the transaction would take place, or if it would even work. We weren't sure if the vessels would accept the souls and comply with what is required, and to some degree, we are still not certain whether the souls will have full control of the vessel, but for now, you seem OK, let's do a check in."

The Collective was powerful, each of us sharing our thoughts, our communication, our pasts and to some degree our presents.

Chapter 13

So, what now, peace calm; I can live my life happily ever after? I know the truth. I know where I came from, what my purpose is and where I am going to, what could be simpler, the lifelong question is "What's my purpose?"
Well, I know what my purpose is, so no more doubt. I am here, I am in my light, my energy, my vessel is compliant, I have now been awakened, now I can crack on with life. Life is going to be good; in fact, life is going to be amazing. This is my life's choice, this is what I believe, well for now it is.

Collective: "I'm sorry to burst your bubble, master, I do hope that you get all of those things in this lifetime, but I'm afraid it's not going to be that easy, this was the first transition."

Soul: "What do you mean?"

Collective: "There are three more transitions, which you must all do to ensure your vessel is fully compliant. The first was getting the vessel to accept the soul the awakening. The second is to remember all of your past lives; more importantly, you need to remember your first life when man was originally created the lifetime where you were connected to the Prime Creator; only in this time did you have the original building blocks of the Renboga. We need you to remember what it was like, how you felt and what skills you had before you were unplugged. Only then can we reboot and rebuild the DNA."

Soul: "Well, that was a long time ago. Why couldn't I remember my first life? That's the most important life to remember, start at the beginning."

Collective: "You remember fragments of lifetimes, many of them are intertwined with other memories, but it's imperative that you remember your first life, in order to lead man into the Fifth Dimension, you must connect yourself with the vessel, remember absorb all past lives, then accept them and then finally it's the rebirth, what you have just done is awakened."

Soul: "Do we have to go through that whole rigmarole again? For all it was beautiful; the end bit was torturous." The vessel part of me was still childlike, filled with fear, remorse, and guilt, I was awake, but bless my beautiful vessel, she was having difficulty.

Collective: "Like we say the first part was a test to see if your vessel was strong enough to comply, the second part is a tad more traumatic on both. The past lives that you have lived have been no bed of roses, they have been testing, trying and sometimes brutal. To take all of this in, you must be 100% committed, otherwise it will not work."

Soul: "What if it doesn't work, what if a vessel won't accept the information at hand, what if they/we are not strong enough?"

Collective: "If the vessel does not comply, then they will pass and another will take their place. We must have 100 vessels to complete the mission, this number signifies the completion of life's tasks, it's the number which is associated with achievements and accomplishments, this is the angelic number of the Prime Creator and Creator Gods."

Soul: "You mean the vessel will die?"

Collective: "Yes, that's exactly what I mean. If the vessel is not strong enough, or if they are tainted in any way, then the vessel will die and another light worker or master will take their place. We have substitutes, just in case this occurs, but we have hope that it won't be necessary."

Soul: "OK, so when does this happen?"

Collective: "It's already happening, Molly."

I was still in my vessel; how could it be happening? Normally, I had to leave my vessel to communicate with the collective.

Collective: "That is why we needed the vessel to accept the soul, to be compliant, so as the souls could communicate without leaving the vessel, it's not always convenient to leave the vessel, nor is it safe."

Soul: "What now?"

Collective: "Now, you need to remember."

My body, mind and soul were thrown into a cascade of fear, as the memories tore from within me. Ripping at my heart, pulling me in to times which had past, did I stay and re-live the life which was? Or do I just observe the scenes before me and remember? Is there any order to this? The lives I can see, appear jumbled, intertwined as though they had occurred together, or simultaneously. I couldn't make sense of what I was witnessing, but faith was all I had. This was part of a greater plan and I had to believe in the mission at hand. I had to reconnect to my first lifetime, and understand the relevance of the last lifetime.

All my lives have led to this one momentous moment, which will change man's way forever. From what I can see, I have been trying to do that in every lifetime. My vessel mind would have been saddened by the number of times it appears I have failed; her young body would have felt negative and low. These memories would have significantly impacted her in a negative way, and probably tipped her over the edge, as she would not have been able to cope with all the apparent failure. Therefore, this is the reason they had the vessel fully accept the soul, like a vessel reset, allowing the soul to take over as a whole; now it was making more sense.

As the pictures became clearer, I could see a pattern in what I was doing, all the times I had failed had been communicated with the Collective. Together we had dismantled the failure, broken it down to better understand why the task had failed, obtained evidence, proof, investigated and identified areas of weakness, then implemented some corrective actions with other souls, which has led us to this day of implementation of the grand plan to avoid the dark forces from taking power.

All my failures and failures of other light workers, masters and soul workers have led to this day. The day which the Collective acted and became part of the earth souls, not only guiding from afar, but were now here on the earth as Guardians of Light with full remembrance of who they are and why they are here. They are only few, but enough to awaken the masters and fulfil the mission, the Creator's great plan. Man is now able to communicate with them directly; this had never been known to man in any era. The light was often hidden in the shadows, rarely showing its hand, it led with riddles, rhymes and prophets who were able to give clues to what the future held, but never gave away too much, leaving man to question the what ifs and whys.

The Collective were information gatherers, watchers, observers; they never got their hands dirty, never got involved. Once ascension takes place, you become member of the Collective, communicating with one voice, you are part of the greater plan of the universe, but what is that plan I hear you ask. The plan is to save man from himself, to reset the button on society.

The Collective has analysed every piece of data, they have come to realise that man's faults are their own, that man's downfalls are ones which they created, as they have submitted to darkness, fear and propaganda. They are about to correct the biggest mistakes of their lives. Millions of souls will be able to better communicate with their light guides. The guides will teach them techniques of how to communicate with the higher selves and become one, the masters will be supported by the Guardians of Light here on earth, their mission is to ensure mankind moves into the Fifth Dimension before the darkness prevails. But never in galactic history has this been known, never have the Prime Creator's light workers been able to intervene in man's lives, never have they been able to communicate directly with man, and never has man be able to recollect his past lives.

This is all new, but the playing fields have changed and now the Prime Creator needs to protect their ultimate creation mankind.

Collective: "From the beginning of time, man was made by the earth in the image of the Prime Creator and the Creator Gods, they were sent to aid and create a brave new world, one with love and happiness, but this was short lived and they were forced to surrender their creation to save the galaxy. The galaxy would have been cast into a galactic war until a compromise was reached."

This was no normal war it was a war which could have ended all civilisations on all planets throughout the universe. This was too big a price to pay for the Prime Creator and the Creator Gods. After all, their planets and their beautiful peaceful races were also under attack and would not survive the weapons used. Thus, the creator Gods communicated with the Prime Creator and agreed to surrender their creation and share it with another entity. The other species was far superior in weaponry, engineering, botany, science, and genetics, they were the ultimate creators, but they lacked one thing that Prime and the Creator Gods had in abundance they lacked consciousness, soul.

"The race was/is controlled by one huge mind, which we believe is nestled in the middle of the planet and maintained by the energy of the planets core. However, the Egoiks had no choice, no freedom to do as they felt, as they did not feel, or question. They had been genetically modified to be this way. They were amazing traders and set a high standard in the galactic market for their creations in trade of new species, or new flora, anything they could tinker with. The Egoik planet was much like earth, abundant with animals, flora, and great oceans and lakes."

Me: "So, what changed? Why did they wage war?"

Collective: "The Egoiks knew they had the superior mind but in order to allow their race to experience choice, they needed consciousness; they needed a soul, and no matter how hard they tried, they could not create this themselves as a soul is a separate living entity which is only generated by love and compassion of its creators. The Egoiks wanted this so badly that they were willing to go to extreme measures to obtain it and only they had the weaponry to fulfil it."

The Prime Creator and creator gods thus agreed to this merger; they all came to a compromise which satisfied all the species involved. The original DNA of man had 12 helixes, these strands would allow man to transcend the human experience, being able to travel in a multi-dimensional manner, whilst communicating with their Gods; however, the Egoiks did not want their species to have this experience, the experience had to be maintained, capped to some degree of control. Thus, the Egoiks tinkered with the DNA reducing the helixes to two-strand DNA, minimising man's ability to live a truly free life.

The Egoiks had never had free will before, and they had never felt love or compassion, so from the day of merging, the two entities have always been at odds with each other. The heart with it is the soul, consciousness, and the mind, which is ego. the Prime Creator was convinced that his heart would always win, truly believing that their creation would prevail against all odds; however, due to man's inability to connect to source, the power and link was lost, only the spiritual masters were able to connect, but to do so, they had to live out of mind and within meditation, therefore relinquishing the human experience which he had been born to experience.

Me: "Why were they not allowed to communicate with their Gods?"

Collective: "Rules were put into place to make this a fair experience; no creator God was able to communicate directly with man, that included the Egoiks. Cascading consciousness into a life of questions, where am I from, why am I here, what is my purpose. Man has never known the truth. Man has felt alone for decades because this is what we agreed; however, now the tables have turned and somehow the Egoiks have got bored of their experiment, no longer tolerating man's free will. They have become tired of mans defiance , and now want to revert man back to the entire Egoik philosophy."

Me: "Which is?"

Collective: "It seems like the Egoiks are doing a planetary takeover, they are controlling man, we do not know how yet, but they are. More souls are taking their own lives, unable to ever return home or reincarnate to live another life. The Egoiks have found a way to create man without soul, to create man in the image of himself. The Egoik soldier who will be activated when the time comes to eradicate any man with a soul, leaving our planets severely diminished as the souls will never be able to return home."

Me: "Holy Moses." That some heavy stuff, my mind was foggy, all the information was a blur, had I dreamt it, or was I awake I was uncertain. I looked around and Bell was still there.

Bell: "How are you doing?"

Me: "What time is it?"

Bell: "It's just gone 4 pm."

Me: "Oh, bugger, I've missed tea, and Fin will be frantic, I'm sorry I have to go, I haven't even mown your lawn."

I jumped up and ran out, waving at Bell as I went. My vessel was jittery, her body felt weird like it was shaking from the inside; it felt like she was going to explode from inside out. I still felt the presence of the Collective, they were there with me. "I thought the vessel had accepted the soul."

"All the vessels have accepted the souls, they have all accepted the information, now we have to see if the vessel can live with the information, or if the mind is powerful enough to fight what is happening and let the darkness preside."

Molly: "How long did the awakening take?"

Collective: "Man has partially awakened before, some of the wisest men on the earth, but never in the history of the earth has a human entity ever awoken whilst remaining in the vessel."

It felt strangely comforting hearing the voice of the Collective in its natural tongue. When they first came to me, they gave nothing away, as they spoke in rhyme and riddles. It was extremely confusing, but I suppose, it was necessary, as they needed to protect their identity. But now I am home, I am back where I belong with my conscious family.

The other souls were silent; there was no chatter, but I felt their energy pulsing through the invisible electrical atmosphere, lifting the vibration of the world.

I returned to my vessel, trying to calm her being, but it seemed to make it worse. The darkness was running through her mind, her stomach was churning, her muscles tightening with painful contractures, her joints and limbs were constricted with little movement, pain writhing through them. Her mind wishing for death to come, when would she see that all she needs to do is to accept the light, relax, Molly, let it happen.

I knew the human body was resilient; I knew it had fight in it, after all every essence is made up of a fine balance between good and bad, then the vessels always have a choice. The bad could be deemed the dark, but it's not, it's just nature; man's instinctive emotions which keep him alive. These have been instilled into man from the day of merging, eat or be eaten, win or be beaten. Man has always had the freedom to choose, even though he thinks his destiny is already determined, it's not true. He can change his destiny anytime; he has choice to be conscious, to vibrate at a higher frequency, yet so many times he chooses to follow the human collective which leads with threats of fear, how do you override these emotions.

How was I going to get Molly to fully awaken? It's not as simple as I thought it would be, but I have noticed one thing which shook me. Molly's heart was protected by a hardened shell, literally, she has shielded herself from so much pain for so long, that the very thing that keeps her alive was failing. Her heart was discoloured grey, its beat was low and slow, I'm surprised this kid is even standing up. How much pain she must have felt to do this to her own heart? What if I have chosen the wrong vessel? What if she dies? Then I ascend, but what about the mission?

Again, more what ifs, even though I am old and wise, and know the past intrinsically, yet I don't know what the next five minutes will do. Molly needed to lay down, but there was no point going back to the house, as she wouldn't find any solace there. I will take her back to the hill, she can lay on the grass, it will be OK. I headed down the lane, going as fast as she would let me, just as I passed the house, I heard a loud voice, as it boomed around me, I felt the vibration of the dark, and knew I needed to get her to refuge before they found her.

I swiftly moved, carrying her with me, I hope it looked like to she was running. I'm sure I'm not meant to do this, but time was running out, and she wasn't fighting no more; her heart was barely pumping. If I knew where she would go, so would they, so I took a chance and went to the land at the side of the stream. This land was owned by two brothers who were fruiters; they grew the most amazing apples, so juicy and tasty, but if they found you on their land, they would chase you with a shot gun. I'm certain the gun wasn't loaded, but it scared the hell out of any trespassers, this was the only chance I had of keeping her safe. I crossed the stream and lay hidden in the undergrowth; judging from the sun, it was just before dusk, and I don't think her father would come down here to look for her, he definitely wouldn't come on this land.

Chapter 14

We lay together, two beings joining as one. You would think that this would occur at birth, and it does to a degree, but the soul forgets everything as it is automatically unplugged from the source of its Creators; however, the soul knows there is something missing and spends a lifetime trying to find their consciousness. It's the most bizarre scenario.

Collective: "Look, you have the power, and you have the skills; you need to heal your vessel before it's too late."

Reconnecting to my source I started the healing process, you would think, I would begin with the heart, but the heart isn't pumping right because of the blockages created by the vessel's ability to self-preserve. The feet had crystallised, the ankles were tight, muscles in the legs had contracted causing black masses of hard muscles, fusing tendons together, her stomach raged with acidic bile, ulcers lay within the stomach wall, angry red tumours attached themselves to the bones which kept up the torso, the shoulders were like concrete with metal rods piercing through, not to mention the arms, again the muscles had formed as black as tar, making it difficult for any liquid to pass through never mind blood.

All these aspects were due to her feelings and emotions, not one good feeling, not one good emotion, she was 14 years old on the outside, but her insides showed the hard life she had experienced. To heal this vessel was going to take a miracle, maybe she was meant to die, maybe we got it wrong, and she didn't go on to do great things. "No, this vessel is right for the mission, ask her."

I forgot I could communicate with my beautiful host, I just took charge, thought she was dying and took over, I didn't stop to think what she would want.

Soul: "Hello, thank you for being my vessel."

Body: "Hello, its OK, I'm glad I can be of some use."

Soul: "Did you know that you are sick?"

Body: "Yes, I am sick of life, I am sick of people who have no consideration for others, I am sick of all the fighting and the pain, I just want to go home."

Soul: "Is that what you want now?"

Soul: "I chose you because of your ability to prevail, you have a strong will and determination. You know there is never good without bad, but it doesn't have to be as bad as you have experienced it. Our species functions at a higher frequency. On our planet, the only emotions we have are love, compassion, understanding and acceptance; this was all we needed. There was no right or wrong, no bigger or better, or more than less, our species accepted our place in the universal cycle, and lived in peace. I can show you how that is done. Would that be OK?"

Body: "Yes, I am up for that, but I don't know how much good I can be. I know what you know; I can see clearly, and I accept it all, but my mind remains my own, and this is dark, I feel as though I am not worthy of anything, let alone saving mankind. People are right when they look at me, I'm worthless, nothing to anyone; all I want to do is for this to end, but I guess you prevented me, because somewhere deep inside, there is light and love. You know what, I don't even think I would know what true love would feel like."

As I listened to her emotions, I knew exactly what she was feeling, and where those feelings had originated from; there is only one place they could have come from. "This isn't you; you are merely a vessel. What you are feeling are the controlling thoughts of the ego; the ego lies in your mind, it is part of the mind and keeps you within the periphery of life. The ego controls you; this is the darkness you feel, and this is another entity within the vessel, you need to absorb the feelings and emotions, accept them for what they are and let them merge into you; only then will they be disempowered, this is the only way. Don't fight it, just accept it, let your inner light diminish its power."

Body: "You are telling me that I am doing this to myself?"

Soul: "No, you are not, believe it or not, you have no power over the ego. You have choice to some degree, but if it doesn't comply with what the ego wants or expects, then you will be coerced to another way of thinking. If the ego ever thinks you are rebelling, it will push back harder with more hurtful self-talk and imaginary scenarios; it will make you believe it is you, but honestly, Molly, it is not you, your true presence is light; you must find a way to reconnect with this and allow me to help you."

Body: "How can you help me; do I not need to help myself?"

Soul: "Love cures all ills; love is the only salvation for any person or any being; the light of love is the one thing the darkness cannot take. This is your true sovereignty, this is where you belong, now you need to reclaim it as yours and shine like a beacon for all other lost souls out there."

Molly: "Well, I think, you are wrong there; the darkness can take love, it can make certain that no host is able to feel love, and without love what hope do we have? My heart aches with the lack of love, my body craves for the hint of love, I seek it wherever I can, but there is little love out there, as when love appears, it is gone without trace. Love is not something which can be held, or maintained, love is an old wife's tale, told by old people, when they reminisce about the old days. How can love cure things when mankind cannot even feel love?"

Soul: "I know your frustration, but you can recall my past lives. You know where I come from, surely, you can feel the loving energy which now resides in you. You have to want to feel this, you and you alone is the only person who can accept this. I cannot make you, the only thing I can do is give you all the love I have, then it's up to you, you can open up your heart and fill it up, or you can let the ego resume its control."

Molly: "So, let me get this right. You will give me love, if I accept it and feel it, I will be healed, to continue to live in this God forsaken world. If I don't accept it, then I will die, taking the vessel with me and you will ascend, and I will go to mother earth."

Soul: "It's not quite that simple, I have told you that you have a choice to be healed and live, or you will die. If you choose to die, I will not ascend, as you will have chosen to die against your souls will, therefore you will be taking your own life and I will not ascend, I will go into the darkness forever, and you will return to the earth."

Molly: "Well, that puts a different spin on things. We came into this world together from the light, we are leaving from the light, I accept your kind offer to be healed. I want to feel love, joy, hope and freedom from the restraints of the hurt and pain I normally feel. Please have my vessel as your own, and heal her."

Soul: "OK, let the healing begin. I love you and I thank you from the bottom of my soul. You are amazing. You are kind; you are beautiful. Let my love radiate through your body, from your toes, to your head; let the loving light enter this vessel and heal what is broken, soften the stony heart, melt the blackened masses, free the contractures of the veins, let the blood run freely through your body, accept my gift to you."

I could feel the toes tingling, as white light radiated through the gaps in the toes, the feet pulsing with the newly charged blood which surged through the widened vessels, from there the light raced up the legs filling each molecule with the light and energy it was created with, the fundamental building blocks of life, each cell was reinvigorated with loving energy. The black masses disintegrated leaving room for the light which was thawing them, the breath became more fluent and not as shallow, helping to pump the regenerated blood around the body. The tumours which were attached to the bones shrivelled and died, leaving the bones as they once were. The loving light worked extra hard in these areas, now for the heart.

The body/mind resisted this area. It was as if she had let me heal every part, but the heart was painful, unwilling to open, unwilling to forgive, unwilling to accept the loving help which was there to help her survive. Tears flooded from her eyes; her body shook uncontrollably. Her sadness poured out of her like a sieve trying to hold water, the mind was controlling the resistance, as sadness and emotion is what appears to feed the ego this was the ultimate awakening, she had to merge with all the negative emotions, accept them and disempower them before the heart could be healed.

Soul: "Listen to me. You are free. You are safe. You are beautiful. You are kind. You are love; listen feel these words, I am here with you, you are safe, I will not let anything happen to you." I know she can hear the words; I know she can feel what I am saying, but it wasn't her resistance was it, it was her mind, her ego.

Soul: "Mind, why are you resisting, why are you not allowing her to be fully healed?"

Mind: "This is my space, this is my area, this is somewhere you have no right to be. You are only the energy source I am the control panel, it's up to me whether or not she is fully healed; you cannot take control of her."

Soul: "Actually, mind, I can take control of her heart, as this was my space, this is where I was placed at birth." As I spoke, I could see everything. I remembered my birth. I remembered where I went and why, and I knew that the heart was mine, the ego had no place here, and this is where I could win. "I am love, I am light and can and will accept anything the ego throws at me, because no matter what I love ego too, I really do; I love everything; I love all, because this is the way we move forward; this is the way we aid man out of darkness."

I was finally there. The heart is the control centre of the body, pumping the oxygenated blood around the body to every cell; without this device, the mind doesn't work, as it needs blood as the energy source, so if the mind keeps inflicting such hurt and pain on its own heart, then the heart will shut down. The mind is the creator of feelings, the creator of all things good, and all things bad. Every action, every feeling and emotion is created in the mind.

Yes, the mind is part of you, but nourished by what it sees and hears in the external world. The mind is the one who falls for the manipulation and lies which the media spouts. It accepts the false truths of others and beds itself into these false narrative, never allowing the heart to experience its own truth, of love, compassion, and empathy, therefore keeping its heart in a constant state of want and need.

The two components were constantly battling for their place; the Egoik mind sought to control its vessel, penetrating the heart with its manipulation and hurt. The heart did not trust its own mind, and would let no one in, the barriers were up and there was no breaking them down, but I am heart, this is my rightful place, and I will heal my home on earth.

I felt much anger, rage and hurt tore through the body, my past experiences, my trusts in mankind, in humanity was all but gone, holding on by a thread, what did I hold in such high regard, why did I choose to return time and time again. I must have had some faith, some trust; I know many bad things have occurred in my life experiences, but I never thought that the body went to such great lengths to protect its vital organs. The body was self-preserving, it was protecting itself, from what?

Confusion writhed within me, the battle between body, heart and mind. I was unable to see clearly to navigate the way of the light, because there was so much confusion, so much manipulation, I needed and wanted calm, I wanted to continue in this life, to finish what I started, but my vessel had to agree to the help it needed.

Soul: "Molly, are you with me, are we going to do this?"
Molly: "Yes."

Her acceptance was all I needed to call in the reinforcements. I know they will be waiting; they are always with me; they just need to be asked for help and the help will be there.

Soul: "Molly, find your breath, inhale, exhale, come on we can do this, we can find the light together."

The darkness was all consuming, the Egoik mind angry and restless, throwing everything it had at us, but all we had to engage was to breath, enter the breath to create a sedate state in which the light could shine. As Molly began to breath quietly and calmly her mind becoming increasingly quiet, no thoughts just calm. The engagement was about to begin to let the light in, let me in. The energy point at the top of the head, called the crown chakra needed to open, allowing the light energy to flow in, which then in return helps to open the other six chakra/energy points, this includes the heart.

We needed the connection to the light as light is information and information can expel the disinformation the Egoik mind feeds the body. Molly just needs to connect to the light; this is the vessel's choice, the body's choice, there must always be choice, so as mankind feels as though he has some control. Without choice, man will be in constant fight or flight mode and this is crippling, to say the least.

The crown finally opened, a white light shot from the sky, into the open chakra and surged through the body. An image suddenly appeared of Fin, the darkness surrounding him. Molly's heart burst free from the shackles of the darkness and let the loving light enter. Her love for her brother resided over everything; her love, the vessel's love not mine, Molly has done it. Her determination to help her brother was far too powerful for the Egoik darkness which sought to control her. In the end, Molly did it on her own, she welcomed in the light.

Her heart was overflowing with the loving light of the Collective and her love and gratitude, as the universal light of the Collective dispersed into mother earth, leaving us to our journey, but always there to give a help in hand. The whole experience was intoxicating. The connection with the divine energy of man, this was man's birth right, this was how man was meant to connect, how they were was meant to communicate, man and woman as one, no division, just love.

Through the light, the portal to the heart was now open and love flooded out, pouring into the body, caressing it like a long-lost lover. The love was rich and warm, each cell vibrated as it awakened and Molly was alive, radiating energy, collaborating with the channel of light.

We were now joined, fully awake and together Molly and me. The loving Collective were masters at unlocking portals, they were the designers, the creators of all portals, the inter-universal planet jumpers, they could do anything if light was the source.

Soul: "Molly, we did it. I know how you feel, so there is no point in asking, but I cannot enter the emotion of the mind, so, how's it going?"

Molly: "My mind is blank; there is nothing there, it's as if he has left."

Soul: "Ah, well, let's just enjoy the peace and quiet and be still, I think we earned it, I thought I had lost you there, I'm sorry it was so tough."

Collective: "Congratulations, you two you have done it. You are now merged and awake, it was quite a journey, we are elated that you fulfilled this part of the mission."

It felt good to be whole. I have never experienced any of this before, for the soul, and vessel to become one, with the fragmented knowledge of the past lives and knowing of where I originated. The age-old question where do I come from, I can now answer that with some accuracy. I come from a star which is in the galactic system of Renboga, my people, the Anuna are the original creators of man, along with the other creator Gods. They have watched over earth and other planets within the galaxy since the beginning of time.

My species had the ability to become pure light, pure energy, which was invisible to naked eye, keeping their existence covert. This secret has been maintained for millions of years. We were the creators of this planet, along with six other species, who were called the creator Gods. The creator Gods had many different talents, sharing their creations equally, they had the ability to make the species conscious. Thus, the Creators shared their energy to create the soul particle and made each being in the image of themselves. Every living being on earth has a portion of a Creator God within them, the flora, animals, and man.

The Creators were not alone in their creation; they also had a counterpart, a part of their planet lived on within earth, as one of the asteroids which created earth came from a dead star of the Renboga Galaxy. The star which had broken apart without warning, taking the Prime Creators partner with it. Therefore, upon creation, the creator gods were saddened by the loss of the Renboga leaders' partner and in her honour, they named the earth in her memory 'Mother Earth' as it holds her conscious energy, along with her creations. The creation of earth was extremely exciting, an opportunity to correct the past mistakes, make a new free world, where all species would be welcome and safe.

This was the great plan of the creator Gods, and they were all in agreement. Earth was a peaceful sanctuary of love and happiness, one which would resonate throughout the universe and uplift the universal energy so as all the planets could benefit. This is just what the universe needed to unite all species and all beings. Earth would become the inter-galactic library for all species a free world for all to enjoy and learn from. Great portals were created around the planet, so as no ship ever had to land, leaving the planet free from congestion. The portals had the ability to transport any species to nay part of the planet within minutes, the Peoples had great powers and abilities using the power of thought to move mountains. Due to the purity of their mind, there was nothing that a Person couldn't manifest.

As earth was taking form, there were many watchers, many species willing it to work and some who became threatened by the creation. The only race which held majority of control throughout the galaxy were the ones who felt they were at risk. There was no reasoning for this, as they were the ultimate creators, engineers, scientist, botanist and geneticists; they were an amazing race who had created the ability for planetary travel, communication, buildings, medicine and many other creations. This race were exceptional, giving their minds to the creation of the universe, so maybe upon reflection, it was understandable that they felt a little peeved when earth was created without them in the loop.

As earth became the trading station of many races, all making their marks on the earth we see today. They freed their minds, creating great nations, monumental buildings, they even became fantastic mathematicians. Races and species were soon learning that they too had the ability to be creators; they too had the knowledge to build, mend and heal. As the species and peoples took form, they became more powerful and took what they had learnt back to their own planets, making them stronger, cleaner, and better able to manage their futures. This was the dream, and it was working; earth was the inter-galactic trade centre of the universe as it had the conscious light which could feed the universe.

As earth grew, the Egoiks watched and observed, growing tired of what they saw; they felt that this was unjust, they were the great creators, and earth was going to be theirs. The Egoiks were not warriors, but they had the technology to end all planets; they had no soul, thus had no compassion for what they were about to undertake. They began a great universal war and purged planet earth into darkness through the great flood, cascading through the realms, dismantling the great portals which connected earth to the universe and made earth their own. They took man for themselves, enslaving them to a world of experiments, man then became their human guinea pigs.

As agreed during the great surrender, the Egoiks placed part of themselves into the minds of men, the ego was created, then man was unplugged from the universal Collective, unable to communicate with their race or species; even the Egoiks were enslaved in the vessel, only leaving upon death.

The remembrance of death awoke me and my vessel. I did a quick body scan, as I did in the beginning, checking my vessel, I giggled slightly to myself, an age-old soul of light in this wonderful young vessel. Oh, we were going to have some fun. Then I remembered my real life, all the dilemmas I needed to face, but honestly, these were nothing in the light of what I have just witnessed. I can do this.

Chapter 15

Fully awake and acceptance of my new self, I bounced up from the dewy grass and headed off to rectify some wrongs, check on Fin and see where mother is up to. If this life is going to mean anything, then it's going to start with the family I was born into. This is the time, right? Just hold on, this isn't normal; no human I know can have a discussion with their soul, so is this right, or am I just talking to myself? Well, obviously, you are talking to yourself, as I am within you and we are one, so yeh, you are having a discussion with yourself. Is that a bad thing? I don't think so, just don't talk out loud, or people are going to think you are weird.

An inert giggle was let out, then we proceeded to the task at hand, family first, remembrance of first lifetime, save human race then ascend. I think that just about wraps it up a nutshell.

Soul: "You are very dry; you know that sense of humour must have got you into trouble in the past."

Molly: "No not at all, I never say what I am thinking out loud, if I think it, I just keep it locked away, I have a private conversation with me, ha ha, but you know that already, so what's new?"

Soul: "I suppose I made the perfect choice, a person who displays as a mute, but converses in her head."

Molly: "I never said I was a mute, you know I'm not, I have a voice, listen."

The sudden scream hurled from my body. My God, it felt good, it felt bloody amazing, all the pent-up energy. I screamed again and again, each time letting more and more energy escape me, the energy poured out of me like a dark torrent falling of a cliff's edge, a powerful waterfall of negative energy releasing from my body. Having all this negative energy pour out of me felt wonderful, a beautiful release. I continued to scream until I had no scream left, leaving me light and energetic, with the power of 20 lions.

My body filled with pure light, all the darkness had gone. All I could feel was love, my heart was full, but I couldn't quite understand what the strange feeling was in the chest. I felt like I wanted to say something, but the words wouldn't come out; it blocked my ability to breath, what was that. The recognition and knowledge of what had happened was acceptable to me as a whole, but now I started to recognise things about my body which I had never noticed before. The way the muscles contract and tense, my ability to breathe or not to breathe, whichever is the case, the sensations within my body caused me to sit for a while, let them subside, then I would continue, but for now, I need to rest.

The sensations in my body, be them good or bad, I can feel each one of them, I can even feel the beat of my heart, which I have to say is a little freaky. So, what to do with my new-found truths? How do I manage the body and the soul? These are all new to me.

Soul – "The soul is energy; therefore, energy can access anywhere, hence why you feel your body, the way it moves, the shift in patterns, the muscles contracting and retracting, all of it, we are pure energy. The best thing you can do is accept, it's not going to hurt you, you are safe, the feelings you are feeling is the energy shifting from place to place keeping your body fit and healthy, its going where it is needed."

When negative energy is released, it will disperse as wind.

Molly – "So, I'm going to go round farting and burping, people are going to nickname me farty pants," that childish giggle was unmistakable, the naivety within me was yet to be tested. I was different, I've always been different, but never quite known why. Now I know why I'm different, but really, I'm no different than anyone else, everyone is in the same boat as me, they all have the same abilities, they can all access the higher sense, they can all listen to their guides, they can all listen to their intuition, they just choose not to.

I was so desperate, so sad that I was willing to do anything for it all to come to an end, for me to finish it there and then. The hatred and hurt I felt towards the people I were birthed to was pure evil, I didn't like them, I didn't like what they represented, or how they spoke, or looked at humanity, I would do anything but agree with them. Their essence of egotistical behaviour which was forged in the shadows, all-consuming with greed and jealousy, which meant none of them could even see the light never mind embrace it. I was at risk of becoming one of them, but I'm afraid I would have ended it before that happened their way was not my way.

I listened to my body and what it told me, how it was feeling and how those feelings normally materialized into something, bad, because nothing good ever happened. My life was a process of bad experiences, birth, childhood and now into adulthood. My family were caught up in their own daily tasks, never having time to listen to me. I was a ghost, a manifestation brought on by man and ignored by man, so the question. "Why am I here?"

Well, I now know why I am here, but it's hard to digest, I am here. I chose to return to this earth plane to save mankind, to save humanity. I am one of the oldest souls from my planet, which has resided on the earth 360 times, some could say I've gone full circle ha ha, I was here at the beginning of time, and have seen how the world has developed and more so how man has developed. Man / humanity is great, they have developed into beautiful, loving, kind and loyal species, where the majority have good hearts and good intentions.

All mankind is made up of an equal balance of energy of good and bad, negative and positive as this charges the world, however there are those few who hold great power and control over the world and over man, having man do their bidding through mind manipulation and subconscious transfusions to make man always want more. Mankind is discontented and thrives to get more, he will do anything to achieve his goal as he is driven by greed and jealousy, thus making man hurt man, turning against each other in the fight for the ultimate power and control.

This is what mankind has become, even though there are those in power who are good with some light in their hearts and wonderful intentions to help develop man into a man, to embrace difference, to embrace each person's point of view. There are those who truly believe in this, and it's those energy sources which will be tapped into, helping to heal the world on a mass scale, bringing earth into the 5th Dimension so as they can break free from the Egoik control.

Collective – The Egoiks have broken the agreement to stay disconnected to man, they have been secretly communicating with certain humans to change the planetary control, now it's time for us to show them that we are not going to allow them to do this. We just need you and the other masters to link us directly with the earth.

This is me in a nutshell, this is what has happened in the last 72 hours, life has taken a whole new path, one which I knew I was on, but couldn't quite get my head around it. So, whilst you're reading these pages, you obviously have questions, and this is my take on it, these are the words from my guides, those birthing souls who were with me when I was born. Those souls who give me the gentle nudge in the right direction, those souls who pass through me as energy causing my tummy to feel tingly or my legs to feel weak, they are communicating with me all of the time, by whatever means necessary.

They are me and I am them, my positive emotions my feelings are conduits to communication. But now I can see them, and I can hear them, albeit in my head, which may sound crazy, and maybe no one will believe it, but it's true, they are all around us, energy sources from other planets, from solar systems.

They are the original builders of the universe, they are the DNA strands which run through our bodies, they are the building blocks of humanity, they are you and me. Can you see? Are you listening? Do you have the ability to listen? Or. Are you just reading their book as an inquisitive reminder of some else's perspective on mankind, evolution of man, humanity, and the world?

You know what, as a soul I absolutely love the world, I love mankind, I love humanity and all that it represents, but as a human those feelings are reversed. I hate myself, I hate mankind, I hate humanity, I hate the world, my perception as a human was "Hell as on earth." This is hell, this is my punishment for doing something bad, all I want to do is to return home, but this god forsaken place keeps pulling me back in, its begging to be saved on an astral level, but on a human level its gross and unkind, unloving, uncaring, cruel to the point of being brutal.

Man is deemed to have evolved over the centuries but has he really, man still enslaves other man, man exploits the opposite sex making them feel lesser than equal. Man hurts the children which are born to this world and trades them for money, putting them into the sex trade, hooked on drugs or as slaves for families who are deemed to be wealthier than others, what man does is ludicrous, and who on earth would want to save him?

But for some reason I do, as this is who man is, for what is deemed as bad, are just actions which lead to emotions, and emotions are those feelings which the Ego feeds on and without them the ego would surely die. So, the only way is to merge with them, disempower them and resume your sovereignty of light, because that is who you are, you are light, created with love. Can you accept what is perceived to be bad, or is there no forgiveness, is there no acceptance, bad is bad and that's all there is to it, send them to jail and throw the key away, or do in return to them as they have done to others, but would that make you feel any better? Whose truth is it anyway, is it your truth, is it your life?

If it was your life, how would this change things, would I be writing these words down right now, or would I be consumed with guilt, or greed, or would I just feel nothing, block it out, so as it can emerge in another life. All the lives I have had are amalgamated into this last lifetime, the hurt and the pain of the past lives, there was little love then, and there is little love now, but this wasn't the grand plan, this wasn't how it was meant to be.

Yes, the soul was meant to have some life experiences in the image of the creator gods, but that was taken from you and instead your feelings have fed the Egoik species for centuries, are you going to continue to allow it, or are you going to resume your sovereign light? They have cheated you repeatedly, are you going to let it continue?

The Egoik Man has caused chaos, created wars, inflicted hurt and pain on others, why because of how they feel, again those negative feelings which impede you from your birth right of love. Can you ever remember a day where you ever felt love?

I think the answer is no, but the collective of the species have learnt that they cannot rule with a collective conscious, they must have purity in the light, and that means awakening to everything, awakening to the good the bad and the ugly, awakening of all lives, so as the soul is whole again. This is where you go when you die, you reconnect to source, you can re-energise so as when you rebirth you do so as a whole.

We become the energy source of our vessel, never knowing where we come from or why we are here, it's like Groundhog Day. Every lifetime is the same, but different as we learn different ways to live, establish alternative methods to experience life. Mankind is continuously learning and feeds into the library of the universe, all other universal species can monitor us, they can see us, visit our planet, but they cannot interfere. So, what do we do?

Collective: "What do you want to do?"

I'm going to get up and go home that's what I am going to do. My mind was powerful, the negative emotions proceeded to pollute the vessel, but the vessel was merging all within, the soul was providing the light and energy source to absorb and disempower the emotions leaving the body to emerge and work as normal. The vessel was running on full power and working like it was designed to work. It was recollecting the past, recording all images and experiences which passed through it with great ease. This was a powerhouse, a working machine, the greatest computer ever designed which could overcome any challenge.

Feeling at one with my beautiful new vessel I felt at peace for the first time in many lifetimes I felt at peace, the energy was surging through me, the luminous colours of each energy point. I not only felt them, but I could see them.

The base of my feet was surrounded by Golden beams of light which inserted deep into the earth, connecting me to her energy. The energy was linked to a Red mist at the base Root Chakra which connected to all other bodily energy points, Orange lit the lower belly Sacral Chakra, Yellow enlightened just above the belly button The Solar Plexus linking and protecting me with universal energy, further up green as we hit the Heart Chakra, blue was communication for the Throat Chakra, then my wonderful third eye a vibrant indigo right in the middle of both eyes my Third Eye Chakra, up to my wonderful Crown Chakra where white light streamed into soaking me with information.

The information streamed in form the "Soul Star Chakra," this is also known as the seat of the soul,' "The Halo Chakra," It is the energy centre of divine love. Clearly remembering the power of this energy point, feeling the knowledge of my soul, and seeing the incarnations I have agreed to and lived. Within this energy I could clearly see the Karmic patterns which have led, and what past incarnations I have held onto and need to release and accept. The past life of remembrance the loss of my children was one of them, but it was not the only one, there were many lives where I have lost, yet I had dealt with the grief with greater ease, why?

As the energy streamed from the heavens filling my vessel and feeding my soul, it felt like I had been starving for decades, awaiting the energy of my ancestral DNA, the ancestral links with my creator. I had always felt a sense of not belonging, or of searching for what? But today I was becoming whole, healing past traumas, transcending this beautiful vessel into pure energy, irradicating hurt and pain. Absorbing the luminous energy which was all around me linking me to all creator's. The soul star chakra was not alone as this linked with the "Spirit Chakra," then the "Galactic Chakra," finally the gateway of Renboga or heaven as you know it, the gateway of home the "Devine Chakra," home.

Feeling all the past wisdom of the ancients the vibrance of the divine. Basking in its strength and power, embracing its true ability, remembering. The energy of home warmed my soul, the loving caresses as my soul withdrew leaving the vessel standing alone, alive and watching, how was this even possible. I am here yet my soul is there. I stood and watched him dancing around, as free as a bird, the humming sound of happiness choired around me. Giggling, I was in awe of the beauty, and this beauty had come out of me, there were lights all around him, differing lights like the ones seen in Havenmoor, he was with his family of light. I could have stood and watched forever, but I didn't have forever, I needed to get home, I was still fourteen after all.

Collective – "Know you can be whatever you want to be, thought creates all, step back and see, thought creates."

As I stepped back, I could see what the collective said, as my soul danced the collective still spoke to me, how can this be? I didn't care how this was possible, I was still connected to my beautiful soul, which connected me to what I was witnessing, my past fears and emotions, not only feeding the ego, but also becoming reality right in front of my eyes, the lifetimes fear reigned, lifetimes of fear. As I witnessed the past fears of divorce, and I got divorced, fear of abuse and I was abused repeatedly, fear of disability and I had a disabled child, fear of difference and I was a witch, fear of being persecuted and I was ridiculed and burnt at the stake. Fear of loss and not having enough, my goodness how much fear can one have, there were all types of fears and each one I had I experienced and had to face.

The fear washed through me, I was witnessing the most horrific lifetimes, and each one I had created due to my emotional state. How could this be so, I have heard people say you are what you feel, yet, I had not taken any notice. Its only now that I am awake can I see what I have done to me, no other person involved, not even my persecutors, as they just played their role, it was me, all me.

I was absorbing all the information placed before me, and as I did, I could see the words of great prophets and wisemen who had been sent before us.

"If constructive thoughts are planted, positive outcomes will be the result. Plant the seeds of failure and failure will follow."

"Everything begins with a thought, and thoughts are turned into plans, and plans to reality."

Finally.

"A man is but the product of his thoughts what he thinks, he becomes." One of the wisest councils born, there is no mistaking his words, as my soul rejoins me, "Mahatma Gandhi."

Beauty and simplicity, he tried to warn the world of the forthcoming threats, he tried to engage with man, but again man did not follow his wisdom, or believe his plight. He was discredited by governments so as no one would believe his words.

I recollect a lifetime where I was on a mission, I had my followers, I had my plan, a plan to overcome my grief and in doing so I would help others. Though the man I had entrusted my heart to sought to take what I had built, as he believed he was more deserving of the role and the honours which were betrothed to my work. He shared my personal trials with the world, casting doubt upon my abilities to think let alone govern my own organisation. All hell broke loose and my fight within the courts broke to the media. His one goal was to break my spirit, to surrender my light so as he could finally shine, even though he put on a good show for the world to believe he was a loyal partner, but I knew the truth, and the information shared by the media had conversations which could only have originated from one place, and that was him.

They smeared my name, with damming headlines whilst communicating some truth within a very sad story. Finally my board got wind of it, even though they knew the truth of the story from my own experience, they would not allow me to speak to the media as they felt it would further damage the reputation I had built, yet the headlines did this on their own. I never stood a chance as the headlines screamed guilt, yet the courts leniency said something else.

At the end of the day I had made a mistake, not an intentional act, yet they chose to hide it like a dirty secret. The story was sensationalised to create hysteria and distrust, though his ploy failed to succeed, despite his many efforts to degrade me, and relinquish me of all my successful endeavours.

I wasn't God, I made mistakes and learned by them, but despite my pain and anguish I never stopped helping people. I never stopped helping those who were not able to speak for themselves. Disability rights and vulnerable people, the passion and power I felt for these children was overwhelming, the love was radiating out of me. Yet after years of trying to resume my position within the organisation I had built, there were those who felt they could do better, be better and achieve more. ? They turned to the one person who sought it all, though they seemed to think they were doing me a favour by approaching him to step in as my aid. Yet they could not see what they were doing, they were ripping the soul from within, and with my blunder they would give it to the one person who had created the false narrative, the monster I called my partner. It wasn't a huge mistake, no one was killed, or maimed, yet he made it feel like the world had imploded because I had failed to manage my own affairs the way I managed the companies. One small oversight did not plunge my creation into a shadow of what it was, instead those that knew me continued to support my venture as they were able to see truth, though to the external world my reputation appeared to be in shatters, as he believed that people only ever chose to remember the bad, as this is what makes him feel good, as he never chose to remember the good in anyone or anything, as he reminded me of this during the many beatings he gave to control me.

Soul – "But you left the organisation on your terms, your failing to see the bigger picture. This was your strength, though the odds were against you, you never gave up, despite the fact that you grew tired, you still had light in your heart. He never got what he wanted, you made certain there was another to lead, and you taught her well."

I fell into a false narrative and blamed others and punished myself, I could feel the pain of the past, the hurt, the disgrace I felt, the humiliation of this past mistake and the regrets. He had sacrificed me like a lamb to the slaughter, to discredit me, so as no other would ever believe my words again, empowering him to continue the satanic beatings and mental torture he inflicted upon me daily.

I had no more fight left in me, Once I had arranged my affairs I bid my farewell at the grand ball leaving a legacy for future generations in the hope that more families and their children would be helped. This was to be my final act of kindness, as Jonah Humphries finally rested and returned home to her family of light.

Captivated by this moment, lost in the memory of the past, I regained the bodily control and emanated the light from within.

Chapter 16

I ran as fast as I could, hoping that this feeling would remain, but it was short lived. Within minutes, the feel-good emotion was gone, and fear, anger and tension reigned. This body must learn how to detach itself from these emotions, from these feelings, they serve no purpose, yet it's what must happen for true enlightenment to ensue. It's up to me to ensure the body stays on track, but I completely understand that this isn't going to be easy; she is going to experience a lot of pain, as the past lives and past emotions channel through her. All my past experiences are now ours, to experience together, and together we will prevail; we will get through whatever life throws at us.

Awakening and merging is the key, just accept the feeling the emotion, the pain, welcome it like an old friend, then let it go with the breath. There is going to be a lot of deep breathing, meditation, reflection. In order to starve the ego, I must first merge with it, disempower it. Then there is going to be the attachment, the attachment of what I had in my past lives, the people I loved and lost, the lives I touched, the people I hurt, the people I loved, all of which I need to release; I need to let go of it all so as I would no longer feed the Egoik mind.

I can let go of all of that, as it serves no purpose to hold it, but? No buts, it's done. I let go of all past attachments; they serve no purpose, the past is where it belongs. I cannot change it, I cannot go back, therefore there is no point in holding onto it. What I must remember is that everyone else has moved on; it's old news, and therefore what is necessary for the world to remember and learn from will be in history books or scribes, or teachings, but what isn't necessary has been forgotten, therefore I must do the same.

This is me; I am love; I am light I am energy; I am pure; I radiate from within, this is the loving light of the universe, this is the loving light of our creators, the Father and the mother. I am part of them for all time, they are my truth, they are my past, present and future, and I will return to Father and leave mother to tend the earth alone. My past lives serve no purpose, other than causing my physical body pain, but we can live through that, it is a small price to pay to return home.

Just as I accept all that is and accept all that will be, I reach home. The cottage glimmers in the autumnal sun, the leaves scatter on the driveway in an array of colour. Just as I step onto the garden, mother shows herself at the front door, and calls me in for tea. I have to say, I felt relieved to see her, she looked lighter than normal, not as old, or haggard. I smiled and nodded in acceptance to her call. I ran inside and for the first time in a long time, there was laughter, there was positive energy, there was family.

I washed my hands and shared in the wonderful energy which surrounded me, even Arty was happy. What had happened? Excited giggles and laughter filled the small kitchen. We all gathered around the table, the feast which lay in front of me was enough for a king, what had happened?

Was this a trick? Was I asleep and this was all in my imagination? You know I have a vivid imagination, holy mosses. My voice found a way to speak, I spurted out. "What has happened, why is everyone so happy?"

Fin was the first to speak up, "We won, Molly."

"We won what?"

Mother looked at me, her eyes were glistening and warmed with love, "I won the lottery sweetheart, all is going to be OK."

My mother always had to depend on father for everything, and this is how he controlled her, how he manipulated her to do his bidding, but now, she doesn't have to depend on him for anything, she has cut all ties, she can finally be free. I looked at father, as he sat there, he looked smaller than normal, less important, and the twist of fate for mother has changed the whole dynamics of the family.

I have never seen mother so happy; in fact, I have never seen her happy, smiling without a care in the world. Well, of course I have seen her smiling, but she always looked grey, like she had the weight of the world on her shoulders. But today, she looks radiant, she is glowing like a beacon in a lighthouse, her light is shining, and she seems free, free from the restrictions placed by my controlling father.

Soul: "Or restrictions placed on herself by her own mind? It is impossible for anyone to place mental restrictions on anyone, unless you let them, so she must have participated in his requests. Its only when you take responsibility for your life, that you discover how powerful you truly are."

My mother came from money, her family were deemed to extremely rich, and she enjoyed the luxury of private school, but she fell in love with the wrong man, which caused her family to cut all ties, locking her out of the family money, thus being totally dependent on father and my golly, didn't he remind her every day. This must have been torture for mother, the mental control, and the physical punishment. Was it what she signed up for?

So, today turned out to be an amazing day. For the first time in my life, I feel calm, the fear has left my body. I can breathe freely and feel confident enough to join in conversation. My short life has been one of fear and retribution, always scared of speaking in case someone takes it the wrong way, scared of looking in the wrong direction in case one of my siblings is looking over and uses it to cause bother, scared to be myself, as I try and fit into this crazy world.

The energy around the dinner table was amazing, everyone was chatting and smiling, the taunts of the day had passed, and mother was home where she belonged. Her seat was at the head of the table, opposite father, yet father could not look at her tonight, it was as if he was not there. This man was somewhere else, probably thinking of a million different ways he can get his control back. I looked at him and felt the shudder run through my veins; this man was pure evil, and I have his blood.

I ignored the small man and continued to enjoy the company. This is probably the nicest evening I have ever had with my family, no jibes, no argument, no freaky outbursts, just laughter and joy which I had never experienced before. Dinner seemed to go on forever, lasting well into the evening. Fin was back to his usual self, laughing and being silly; he looked like he didn't have a care in the world, and the woes of the past few days had been forgotten. In fact, it was as if the family had always been this way, it felt so natural, and beautiful, like a little piece of heaven.

This is how I want to live the rest of my life, happiness, and joy, letting go of all the fear and apprehension, letting go of the past. I'm still not certain if I can merge with all my past afflictions and lives, the hurt and pain in this life alone is enough, but if it is what I must do then, this is worth the fight, and maybe, just maybe all mankind could live the way I have experienced this evening, where the feeling of being abundant in every way is enough. How can being abundant make you feel love though? Why does money even come into it?

Soul: "Wealth is a form of control, most people don't have enough to pay the bills or live, which means they live in constant fear."

Molly: "Take mother, for instance, she used to get a total of £150 per week to feed and clothe seven children, how was that even possible? Birthdays, Christmas, were always sad times for us as we rarely ever got what we wanted, or even worse, we asked for nothing at the fear of an argument. There was always retribution. If you asked for something, you always had to give something back in return and the price was normally too high, but mother constantly had to ask for more, as she didn't have enough to feed us. I figure her retribution was a beating, but after today, there was going to be no more beatings, no more control and father can just go and climb back into the hole he came from."

Whilst in this state of mind, I could feel my body; it squirmed within me, like leaches or thick black slugs sucking at my blood, they are stuck to my insides sucking the life out of me. I can feel them, what is that? And no sooner did I ask than my inner self knew the answer. "It's the past, the past lives the past emotions, the past feelings; the only way to release them is to welcome them in, let them merge with you, disempower them."

Molly: "Jesus Christ, is this what it is going to be like? Recognising all this pain, living in all this pain, they are going to eat me alive, I can feel them; they are everywhere, in my arms, my legs, my back my shoulders, and one huge one is stuck to the left of my spine."

My soul was with me, we were combined, it knew what was happening, and kept reminding me to breath and merge, but my mind was screaming, even though I was extremely happy and very calm. These emotions were like talons trying to drag me down to the depths of despair, they were reminders that I can be taken at any time by negative emotions, and this was my fight. I looked at every one and saw the light shining all around, this was worth fighting for. I turned to mother and asked to be excused, I just needed to be alone.

Mother smiled, then held out her arms for an embrace. Feeling her arms around me, melted everything away, the negative emotions, the leaches inside, everything dispersed, love will be the saviour, then she went on to say, "Love you up to the sky and over the rainbow." I smiled and said, "Love you too, mother."

It felt strange hearing my mother say, "I love you." This wasn't her usual demeanour. I'm more used to ducking than loving. Could all of her spiteful and hurtful words have come from not having enough, disappointment, or the hurt she felt inside? Was I her outlet, the one she blamed for how she felt? The hurt raged within me, the doubt cascading through me, was this who mother was meant to be? How can you hurt a child which you had birthed? How can you do that, why would you do that?

Soul: "Of all the lifetimes I have had, there has been one commonality and that is fear. Greater the fear, more anger was within as man never knows where the fear comes from, and neither did I until now. I wasn't able to understand the past lifetimes, the hurt and pain, but now I know that I wasn't in full control, it finally makes sense."

Finding my comfortable position in the lounge was bliss, the lounge was warmer than usual as mother had turned on the fire, the red and orange hews lit the darkened room, giving it a magical feel. Reeling from the true doubt of mother's love, I gathered my thoughts, balanced my emotions, and sought my truths yet again. The day had been long, my bed was beckoning, but night time was still young.

Why didn't I stay with my family around the table, why didn't I just enjoy their celebrations? It felt as though the whole house had been lifted, and even though I was happy that they had found peace, solace from the retribution of father. I knew there was still a lot of work to be done on me, to get this body to feel and accept peace. My main aim was to help this vessel survive the traumas of my past lives; the only way that was possible was to remember my first lifetimes, the life where ego did not exist. The time before the threat of another great galactic war, the time where man still had a connection to the Prime Creator and creator Gods. This was what I had to remember, then maybe I can help reverse the Egoik tinkering of man's DNA, find a way to rebuild or restructure them, so as every man can become what he was born to be. An inter-galactic species which held the secrets of the universe, was able to transcend the physical dimensions and enter the safety of the Fifth Dimension where we can regroup our species.

My past lives used the vessel like a dumping ground, all the rubbish I have experienced is now held in this one place, and in order to overcome the submission of the emotions, I need to remember how it once was, my original lifetime when the Peace ruled. I needed to remember the time where love prevailed above and beyond all else, where ego had no place. Tears welled in my eyes and my heart felt heavy, the hurt and pain of what was. The past has a lot to answer for, but it's made me the soul I am today, the wisdom which I hold cannot be questioned, yet I find myself skulking behind others, hidden and afraid to come out, what the hell I am doing?

Frustrated by what I felt, my mind was screaming to be heard, but my heart told me everything I needed to know. The purity was fighting to be released, it didn't matter if I was hidden, at this time that was OK. I will have time to shine when the time comes, I will step up, but for now I need to heal. This is my time to awaken and to embrace all that was happening, and all that was about to come, my guides were with me; they would not leave; I knew I wasn't alone, the other light workers and masters were awakening too, this was our time.

I just needed to quieten my mind, so I could hear my heart, the soul was calling to me, reminding me of where I came from. Yet the body was still controlled by the Egoik mind each were fighting for position.

Collective: "Calm yourself, don't let fear guide you, we are here right by your side."

Soul: "Yeh, I know, I am trying, but the ego is far more powerful than we know, and it feels as if it is growing, it's getting stronger, no matter how I merge and disempower it."

Collective: "What do you mean it's getting stronger, that's impossible?"

Soul: "I am telling you, it is getting stronger, whatever we are doing it is fighting us, like the body fights a virus, the ego is fighting me, its fighting the vessel."

Collective: "We have studied the ego for thousands of years. When the Egoiks merged themselves with mankind, they changed the DNA so as man would be unable to communicate with the Creators or the Egoik creators, nor would he recollect the past. This put man in a grave situation; the soul would become the prisoner in the vessel, never knowing their ancestors."

Soul: "Why do we then choose to be reborn? Why even bother coming to the earth, if we are choosing to be in prisoned in a vessel which has no way out?"

Collective: "Earth is the greatest test and even though it has the restrictions, it is still a free-will world; there is no interference by any species, man must be left to choose his own path, the only aid is guidance, but majority of men don't have the ability to listen to spiritual guidance, as they are better comforted by the negative emotions created by ego. Sadly, man's comfort of another's demise or another's downfall is strong, it feeds man's ego, leaving the soul starved of affection and love. Hence, the souls are dying, or worse, they are being terminated and the ego is reigning, but this cannot continue as too few souls are returning home."

Soul: "Do you know how messed up that sounds? Souls are born into man into fight he can never win, the only time he has solace is the time between births, why do we even bother?"

Collective: "You bother because the greatest part of you is from the Creator Gods; you know what it is like to live in peace and harmony, you and the other masters have the ability to lift earth into another realm before the Egoiks completely submersed the earth with its Egoik control."

Soul: "How do we do this? How do we conquer a part of ourselves, as it's here it's listening, it's within us, and the closer I get to understanding it, merging with it, feeling its presence the more it rebels? I think maybe the Creators got it wrong, and in this agreement with the Egoiks, the Creators should have had the soul placed in the mind, the mind is the brain, the brain is the control panel, we got it wrong."

Collective: "The collective, your family are peaceful people; they are watchers of the universe, as are the other Creator Gods, as they reside in love, they felt that to place to soul in the organ which kept the vessel alive would be the most important, as the vessel can still breath with machines without mind / brain/ ego, yet it cannot without heart."

Soul: "Yeh yeh, I get that; I get why the soul was placed there, but do you know how hard it is to access, how hard it is to feel with the heart, the mind is extremely powerful, and the ego doesn't seem to mind sacrificing the vessel for its own purpose."

Collective: "But the ego cannot live without mind, as this is what keeps it alive; the ego resides in no other place, it cannot live outside the vessel like you can; it is not energy, it is part of the Egoik creation; it is part of their collective mind, unplugged from the central mind, mans egoik particle feeds their central mind it is indoctrinated to follow, no matter what the outcomes, it will sacrifice anything to succeed, even its vessel."

Soul: "Woah, what the heck are talking about? Where does the mind go to when the vessel dies?"

Collective: "We don't yet know that it is not linked to the soul. The soul returns to Havenmoor; some souls get stuck on earth and remain in the gap in-between, unable to leave, and some return home to their planet of origin."

Soul: "Yes, I get where we go. I remember that part of it; in fact, more memories are flooding back all of the time. But what I don't get is how ego is fighting me, the soul, and winning to some degree; it is hurting the vessel. Her body is abused as it tortures her from inside out. Do you know how the ego twists the stories of the past? I recollect them in purity, the love, yet the ego is distorting them, it is hurting the vessel, it is not our awakening which will kill her, it's the ego."

Ego: "No matter how you try, you will not resume control over her. I am the great controller; I am the mind, the mind always runs the vessel, and you are merely the pumping station, you're in above your head and you will not win."

I could hear the whispers of the Collective, but if I could hear them, so could he; he knew the plan, and was counteracting every step of the plan. The ego was far more astute than I imagined, but who had control? The mind was part of the vessel, as was the heart. I resided in the heart, but I had no place in how he worked. I presume that's the same for the mind, the ego is merely a visitor in the vessel, or is he actually the mind?

This was too complex even for me. Yes, I am a master, I have been here for many lifetimes, albeit I have never experienced anything like this.

Collective: "The ego cannot hear us, as we only talk to our souls, directly to the soul, there is no mind involved. Remember at the monastery, what did you have to do with the mind to communicate with us?"

Soul: "The mind was still, no thought, hence why I could hear you, feel you, but now I am not in meditation. I feel like I am in fight or flight mode, I can feel my beautiful vessel, the pain she feels is indescribable."

Collective: "Yes, we know, you just need to keep her energised, the power of light will compensate for anything the ego can throw at her; if you can shut the mind of decompartmentalise for now, to keep the vessel alive, you have had the training, you know how to do this, we need time to work out how the ego is getting stronger."

Chapter 17

Body: "I can hear all that goes on from both sides, I am the vessel and I know all. You have both used me and treated me like a human punch bag. My body is physically breaking down; my soul is accepting and merging trying to save me, and the ego is lapping it up, yay, control over the master. The ego is inflicting as much pain as he can, without killing me, but I know that if it comes to it, then the ego will sacrifice me, rather than dispelling its secret. This is the way ego controls; it would rather kill its host and kill itself than allow the Collective to learn how the ego is gathering its power."

The only thing which was keeping the vessel afloat was a remembrance of long ago, the remembrance written into the code of my DNA, the story of the snake, the snake which crawled over to a sharp saw and was cut. In anger, the snake wrapped the saw with its thick body and proceeded to squeeze the life out of the saw.

With each squeeze, it felt more pain, but it continued because it wasn't going to let the saw get away with the pain it caused. The snake, refusing to let go of the saw, eventually died; not knowing the whole time, he needed to let go of the initial pain and focus on the future and where it was going.

Instead, the snake unfortunately, lost its life and didn't even see it coming.

This is the analogy of the ego; the ego places so much fear and causes so much pain on its hosts, it doesn't realise that in turn, it is killing itself, its consumed with rage, and wants to persecute its host for the pain it feels, as the pain breeds fear and fear feeds its creators, as it takes all the light. Thus, ending in darkness, no light at the end of the tunnel, just retribution, but for what?

Body: "This whole process has been like a dream, I don't know if I am experiencing anything, or if I am just dreaming it in my mind. I don't know what is real and what is not, but what I do know is that mankind is in trouble. It doesn't matter what the Collective told my soul, I can feel it, I know it in my bones that something bad is about to happen. I suppose I have known it all my life, that innate fear, its unmistakable, the animal instinct of survival, the fight or flight mode."

The initiation process of the introduction to light seemed easy, but they said it would become harder, and to recollect the first lifetime before ego was implanted, all of that I can relate to, what I can't relate to is the three-way conversation I am having in my own body.

The communication, between the host/vessel (Body), the soul (Heart) and the ego (Mind), all battling to be heard, all battling for a place, which one would win? Well, I suppose I am in charge and it's up to me to define what I want; it's just the pain of it all which causes me uncertainty, as I want the pain to stop, but it cannot stop until my body is cleansed and this may take a while. The concerning part is that 30 minutes on the earth plane is a year in the galaxy as time replays faster there. So, I could spend the next 30 or 40 years on this mission, it will take over my entire life and for what?

To have them observe, to have them watch us tear each other apart, the selfish attitudes of mankind, the greed and the feeling of never having enough, we are never satisfied we always want more, but what is it all for? Frustration rises, I know my mission, my purpose, why I am here, I know where I am from, yet the limitation placed on myself, the physical host is debilitating and restricting; every sinew, every muscle, even my organs feel like they want to burst out of my body, as they scream for release, so how to move forward.

Collective: "Each day will bring new challenges, but for now, you move forward with the knowledge of where you are from and why you are here; you know what is asked of you, after all, this has been your soul mission every lifetime, you are part of the Prime Creator and creator Gods, you are Pleiadean watcher, from Anuna we know you will achieve your goal, family first, then raise the planet to where it was originally born, love and light will resume."

Collective: "The Prime Creator and creator Gods have abided by the agreement forged with the Egoiks thousands of years ago, but the Egoiks have broken that agreement; they are now communicating with their creation."

Soul: "Is that why you are communicating with me? Is that why we have been awakened?"

Collective: "Yes, we have never interfered in the lives of man. We have guided from afar and man has got close a few times, but we are not allowed to communicate directly, as this was the agreement. Man is a huge experiment, man has some great abilities which he chooses not to use, we needed to see how it would pan out."

Soul: "What do you mean man has some great abilities?"

Collective: "Man can create his own reality; his thoughts can create, his thoughts are his actions, his fears, and desires. Man can create whatever man chooses."

As the Collective spoke, I remember a lifetime where I recollected that experience. The lifetime where everything was just perfect; I had money, success, a wonderful family, I wanted for nothing. Love surrounded me, it engulfed me in its vibrance, the life was beautiful, it was peaceful, as I lived in an old province with cobbled streets; everyone knew everyone, the whole village was alive. I lived and died at a good age, surrounded by family. What did I do differently in this lifetime? Ego was still with me, as it never left, yet I cannot remember feeling one ounce of fear or sadness in this lifetime. In fact, I remember many lifetimes where creation was the conduit to happiness, peace and longevity.

Is that the key? Is creation the key to appeasing the Egoik mind, the lifetimes I created I was at peace, the lifetimes I was a writer, a painter, designer, these were the lifetimes the ego did not intervene, not even in youth. The Egoiks feed from the light leaving only fear, hurt, pain, could it be that they also feed of creation, which would leave them to be peaceful?

I could hear the Collective discussing my realisation, mumbles as they all spoke at once.

Collective: "We agree that this could be a possibility to better understanding the Egoiks and their feeding rituals, but it doesn't answer the question why they have started to communicate with the egos directly. After centuries on the earth plane, why have they changed now? The only way we can protect our souls is to reside without ego, restore the original DNA from the Creators and create another dimension where the Egoiks cannot enter."

I could hear no more chatter as the silence broke, I returned to the kitchen where I could hear the clutter of pots and pans; my two sisters stood there washing at the sink, this made a welcome sight; the cynic within me figured they wanted something, but that was OK with me. I was just happy that I wasn't doing the pots again. A smile rose within, and a merry skip released from my legs as I opened the door to the living room.

The energy within was beautiful, the room was full, all the family were home, sitting chattering about the future. Mother was redesigning the house, excited about extensions, bedrooms, upholstery and colours, she was asking each of them what they wanted and how they would like their bedrooms to look. Father sat on the couch, I had never seen him sitting before, he was always lay down, leaving no space for others, but today, he had no choice, as he was no longer needed, and he no longer had power over any of them, even Arty.

The conversations went on until they were conversed out. Mother asked Erbie to go to the shop and get some crisps for supper; we never had crisps, this was a real treat. Erbie jumped up, with optimistic eyes and asked for the money, Mother went to the brass bin at the side of the fire to get her purse, she always hid it there hoping that father didn't know, but hey presto, the money was gone!

Oh well, never mind mother said, we will eat some hot toast and butter, and I will do some coco, anyone want some? We all quickly went to work helping her gather all what was needed. Fin got the bread, Nessa the cups, Immy put the milk on the hob, Jay got the butter out of the fridge, the humming noise of happiness was delightful, each of them had their place and all were happily getting along. Well, nearly all, Arty held back and sat with father; I could hear them whispering, sniggering, but chose to ignore it.

Mother toasted the bread under the grill as it fitted more slices than the toaster, whilst Jay was busily buttering it. Mother went and put the coco into the pan, along with a heap of sugar, then Immy poured the coco evenly into mugs. All were placed on the table, and we hurriedly took our places, Fin was smiling, he has an excited energy, and even Erbie sat at the table, he didn't talk but his eyes were wide open with the wonder of what was happening.

Father and Arty chose not to join in the festivities; they stayed in the living room, probably plotting the demise of the happy occasion, but for now, we all decided to ignore them and share in the celebration of mother's win. Mother sat in her usual spot at the head of the table and looked at us all, the sincerity shone through. Then out of the blue, she asked, can we all join hands? We all did as she asked, and she bowed her head and gave thanks for her win of £10,000,000, she thanked her mother and father and the light around her.

I sat, listened, and breathed, then said amen; we all said amen, it was a beautiful moment. Mother had never given thanks before, she wasn't a religious lady, yet something that night had compelled her to say thank you and share that gratitude with us all. Once supper had finished, we all shared in the cleaning up; each one of us cleaning up our own area, not one person was left to do all. We all chatted together as one, as it should be, there was no arguing, no name calling, it was as wonderful.

I stood back and just witnessed the scene, how could winning the lottery have such an effect on a family? I appreciate that money is a necessity, but does money come at the price of love? Can money buy love?

Collective: "Money cannot buy love, but what it has done tonight, it has given your mother freedom to leave the control of your father. She had no money, seven children and no means of keeping them without your father; now she feels free, because she no longer needs his money, his house, his transport, she now has choice and freedom to do what she wants to do."

Soul: "Yeh, but she could have left him before, we would have managed, it would have been OK."

Collective: "That isn't a chance your mother would take with all of you, the cost would have been too great, and housing is not easy to come by; she would have had to give reason to why she left, and she is too proud for that, there is no way she would admit the beatings."

Soul: "Yeh, OK, point taken." My 14-year-old self couldn't get my head around it.

Collective: "You need rest, there is lots which still remain unresolved, and you must fulfil the mission, just have peace within that your family is OK, and they are doing well, that is one less thing for you to have concern about."

Soul: "Yes, OK." Reflection is a good thing, as I took a minute to reflect upon the day's events, woah, what a day, and it's all ended OK, so sleep was beckoning, and I couldn't wait to fall into a loving slumber.

Mother was stood at the sink; she looked happy, so I didn't disturb her thoughts. I just whispered good night in my head, she must have heard me though, as she shouted. "Night, night, god bless, love you up to the sky and over the rainbow."

As I smiled and shouted, "Love you too, thank you."

For the first time in fourteen years, I went to bed happy and confident, for the first time, there was no weight upon my shoulders. I wasn't even scared of bed, normally that terrifies me, sleeping all alone, waiting for the darkness to take me, but not tonight, all was good, in fact all was amazing.

As I awoke from my slumber, I heard the muffled voices, the cries of innocence, as I emerged from my bed, my body felt robust as if it had grown a foot. I felt taller and stronger, yet I was not. As I passed the mirror, I could see the energy which surrounded me, bright blues, yellows, gold and white engulfed my aura. The wisdom was calling to step forward as the 14-year-old me struggled with what I was about to find.

I lifted the latch on the old door and stepped inside. Never had I been into my parent's room during the night; it was a taboo area, one which was to be respected by children and never entered into unless invited. Thus, knowing that what I was doing was wrong, I needed to see for myself. I lifted the latch ever so slowly, yet it sounded like a bomb had exploded in my head, I peered around the door and there he was!

The small man was knelt on top of her, I could see her hands flaying under his knees, grasping for whatever she could hold, his grunts of despise were upon her. "Who the hell do you think you are? You are nothing without me, I will ruin you. You will end up with nothing, I will disgrace you, who will believe you? You will sign the money over to me." As the words were pouring out of his mouth, his fists were punching her in the ribs, his fingers were nipping her busts, he was clawing her, punching her, doing whatever he could to hurt her. I could see her face as the moon hit her cheeks lighting up the tears which silently fell. She would not reveal her secret; it would shatter her pride and that was all she had left, instead she would give into him, she would concede to his needs. But not anymore, I would not allow it.

Disgust raged through me. I wanted to end this evil which persecuted my mother, this was no more. I stepped through the door, and he did not see me until I was stood right in front of him. His face was fierce, eyes red with anger, lips pursed with resentment. He looked at me but did not stop, he was defiantly provoking me to react, but I did not, I just watched. Why was I watching? My mother could see me there, she fought for him to stop, now she had something to fight for, her secret was no more, I knew.

I watched my mother, I could see her energy supporting her, blues, yellows, pulsed around her, but it wasn't enough, she needed help, but I could not intervene as this was her battle one which she had to succeed herself. She had to find the fight within to be triumphant, yet he was goading her, still clawing at her body, punching where he could.

Why wasn't I helping? How could I stand and watch? I was a child. What could I do? But I was also a master, wise beyond years. I stood and bloody watched. Infuriated by what I was seeing, how could I not help, why was he not stopping, he was looking straight at me, could he see me? I stepped forward to grab his hand, but my hand went straight though. I was ghost, flipping heck, I had bloody died, and no one had told me! My God, I can go home now, I turned to leave, but I couldn't, my feet were stuck unable to move left or right, I was witnessing an horrific event, and I could do nothing.

"What the hell was going on?" My mind was screaming.

And then, yes you got it, the Collective spoke. "You are witness to your mother's demise, what are you going to do?"

"Are you joking? What the hell do you want me to do? I can't physically stop him, obviously, I'm not in physical body, what would you have me do."

Collective: "Remember where you came from, remember your light, how do you help another's plight."

Oh, flipping heck, here they go again with the rhymes, it's a bloody nightmare, that's what it is, I'm not 'really' here, I'm dreaming.

Collective: "Feel with your soul, the love within, feel this now, and let's begin. You can save your mother, you know you can, this is your path you need to save man."

So, who am I saving, mother or man, again with the riddles, Collective: "Life is but a riddle, for your exploration with you in the middle."

I turned to see if he was still beating her, the pillow over her face, how the heck was he keeping that on her face and using his hands at the same time, his knees held her arms, what held the pillow? I could see nothing holding the pillow, it was just lay over the side of her head, tears had stopped falling from her eyes, as I looked, I could see nothing, she was no longer fighting, she was dying!

What the hell!

Collective: "It's not too late for her to be saved, the path in front she has paved."

Right, pull myself together, how the heck, I needed to remember then I could save her. I fought hard, trying to remember, but there was nothing, the pain I felt inside as a child, the hurtful words she has spoken resonated with me and hurt me more, how could I overcome the pain I felt of her hurt?

I was more than that, I could overcome it. I was pure of soul and I was not about to let my mother die. I had a choice. Love radiated around me, linking with my birth mother, I gave her all my love.

He had stopped punching her and began shaking her, he knew what he had done. His face was white, his repulsion and spite poured out of him as he hovered over her, whispering her name, to no avail, she was not responding. Without hesitation, he stood up turned and put on his trousers, leaving the corpse to take her final breaths. There was no remorse; there was no guilt, in fact, I felt nothing from the man who stood before me. As he stood, he began to laugh, laughing within, as stifled mumbles, the smirk was held on his face.

I was going to wipe that smirk right of his face.

I connected with mother's energy as we met in Havenmoor, the land in-between.

Mother: "So that's it, he's done it this time."

She looked younger and freer than I had ever seen her, the true essence of her nature, though she was not Anuna or Pleiadeans, her vibrant red hair and emerald green eyes glistened as she listened.

Molly: "It's not your time; you must return, you still have work to do; you cannot give up, you need to face this, then you can ascend like you should."

Mother: "I like it here, its peaceful. I am calm, I don't want to go back, I don't want to live like that anymore. Do you know how long I have yearned for it all to end?"

Molly: "I do know that feeling as I was the same, yet here we are."

Mother: "Hold on, I know why I am here, but why are you here, how?"

Molly: "That's a long story, but you must go back, I will help you."

Mother: "How can you help me?"

Molly: "Just let me try, you once sacrificed your life to carry me, so let me do the same for you. Your life has only just begun, you have an amazing future, you will do wonderful things, let me help you."

Mother's face softened, her eyes were humble, she knew she no longer had to fight, her life was going to be OK. She nodded.

With all the love of the universe, help me, help my mother, I call upon the universal energy of the federation of light, fill me with the power to engage the light of mother.

Nothing, really!

Mother: "Well, that worked." She giggled like a child, as she wasn't that bothered about returning, so it was OK that it didn't work. We stood and laughed, and laughed, each accepting what had occurred. Then as the laughter poured out, the light surrounded us both, the blinding light of the universe, rising from the earth, besieged by the light we both were in free fall.

With an enormous flash, we were home, mother gasped as father was just about to leave. He turned in horror at the sound. "This couldn't be. you had stopped breathing; you were gone." Shaking his head, stepping towards mother, but he could go no further as the energetic force repelled him, he pushed and prodded to get closer to her. His anger welled up inside him, he was enraged.

"How?"

Mother just smiled, got her phone from the bedside cabinet, and called the police. He could do nothing; the protective barrier would protect her whilst she took action. As she spoke, she held her voice with purpose and told them all they needed to know. As she spoke, the little man gathered what he could into a bag and was gone, cursing as he moved. There was nothing he could do to hurt her anymore, she was protected by the universal light, but I am certain that isn't the last we have heard from him, he will be back.

The next thing I knew the sun was warming my face, the side of my mouth was sticky where I had slathered, and my limbs felt loose and pain free. The house felt lighter, cleaner, and more energised than it had ever felt. I smiled as I knew we had succeeded, there would be no more hurt or pain in this home, the future was theirs to make their own. They now had a chance, so let's see how it goes. Now, all we have to do is replicate it to save mankind.

The 14-year-old me giggled as I dressed, and for once in this short life, I was finally happy.